MEL ARRIGHI

Alter Ego

QUARTET QRIME

First published in Great Britain by
Quartet Books Limited 1984
A member of the Namara Group
27/29 Goodge Street, London W1P 1FD

First published in the United States of America
by St Martin's Press, New York, 1983

British Library Cataloguing in Publication Data

Arrighi, Mel
Alter ego.
I. Title
813'.54 [F]   PS3551.R7

ISBN 0-7043-2414-8

Printed and bound in Great Britain
by Mackays of Chatham Limited, Kent

Quartet Qrime

ALTER EGO

Quartet  Qrime

ALTER EGO

1

My editor is a hard man to persuade. Give him sweet reason and he comes back at you with "the bottom line." Promise him the extraordinary and he deflates that promise with "the bottom line." And for Norman Wagstaff, as for almost every other executive in paperback publishing, the bottom line is just one thing: a likely profit.

Still, I had a lot at stake—more than Norman could ever guess—and, letting my coffee go untasted, I persisted in my pitch.

"Believe me, Norman," I said, "this new character *will* sell. It may take a book or two—it usually does—but then he'll catch on. He *has* to—with his wit, his style—"

"Wit. Style," Norman repeated sourly. "What do the frecklebellies know from wit and style?"

He took a quick, savorless swallow of his martini. Before lunch, Norman had had a prudent spritzer. But now that I was into the heavy business, now that, in effect, I was threatening him with the loss of his most successful mystery series, he had suddenly switched to the hard stuff.

"Maybe I don't want to write for the frecklebellies anymore," I said. "Maybe I want to find a different audience."

"So go ahead and find it," Norman said. "Write a story for *The Atlantic Monthly*. But give *me* another Biff Deegan. Please, Hank."

There was genuine pleading in his voice. And the look on his toy bulldog face reminded me of a look of the actual toy bulldog I once had owned—the confused, hopeful expression it would have when I would pull away a bone, and it would look at me for some assurance that I hadn't really meant it, that I was about to deposit the delectable thing between its paws, after all.

But I wasn't ready to give up. I didn't see Norman that often—this lunch at Le Perigord was my first face-to-face meeting with him in months—and I had to make the most of it. It was my chance to change the direction of my career. And save my sanity.

"You still haven't told me," I said. "Just what is it you don't like about Amos Frisby?"

Norman's eyes widened. "Who?"

It occurred to me that I had yet to mention the name. "My new series hero."

"Oh." Norman seemed to contemplate the name—with no great happiness—then, very gently, he said, "Well, he's too special."

"What's wrong with special?"

"There's nothing wrong with it, as such. Special can be nice—special can be well reviewed—but special means fifty percent returns. We don't publish books to have them sent back to us. That's the bottom line."

"No book of mine gets returned."

"No Biff Deegan novel, you mean. Let us not lose sight of reality. It's Biff Deegan they're buying. Not Hank Mercer."

"That's a pretty fine distinction, isn't it?"

"You know what I'm saying." Norman spoke with the

practiced patience of an editor who has had to spell out the obvious to many an obtuse author before. " 'Amos Philby by Hank Mercer' just wouldn't be the same thing."

"Frisby. And I know there's a market for such a character. Not a mindless gorilla but a man of intellect—elegant, erudite, tasteful. . . ."

"You don't say," Norman murmured with mock wonderment. "Funny, I've been in softcover publishing for twenty-eight years and I haven't found it yet. Hank," he asked wearily, "why don't you just stick with Biff Deegan?"

"Because I don't *like* Biff Deegan," I said. "I don't *relate* to Biff Deegan. I happen to think there are other ways to solve a crime than kneeing somebody in the groin!"

I had said it with feeling, somewhat more than I had intended, and my voice had risen sharply. The three people at the next table all looked at me at the same moment.

I had been halfway aware of them all along—the young woman in particular—since they were in my line of vision. The two men were angled away from me, but the woman was facing me. She was slender and beautiful, and I would have thought she was a fashion model—the exotic Parisian type, not the wholesome American variety —if it hadn't been for a peculiar seriousness about her, an air of gravity that suggested intelligence and, at the same time, concern over some deep problem. She was dressed sedately in a gray three-piece outfit, but her dark hair was cut in an eye-catching geometric pattern of close-fitting, inverted flaps. Two small triangles were at the back of her head and two large triangles were at the sides, with the apexes hanging just below her ears.

Her male companions turned their attention back to her immediately, but the young woman kept looking at me. I gave her a quick little smile to apologize for my boorish outburst. She didn't smile back. She gazed at me with strange intensity. It was almost as if she was trying to communicate something to me.

"A kick in the balls is commercial," Norman commented.

"Norman, are you really that cynical?" I asked. "I mean, is that *all* you want to do—appeal to the worst in people?"

"I wouldn't put it that way," he replied. "But I'm not paid to provide moral uplift, either. And Hank," he added mildly, "let me remind you, *I* didn't create Biff Deegan."

"No, I did. I take full blame for it. I've written eleven books featuring that big ape—and do you think I'm proud of it? I've had Biff beat up the bad guys in the most sadistic ways I could imagine. I've had him screw every woman he could get his paws on. And I've lost count of how many people I've had him blow away with that .357 Magnum."

"Lots," Norman said appreciatively. "Biff Deegan has done well by you, Hank."

"By your house, too."

"You bet. And he's doing better than ever," he went on. "*Death Is My Bedmate* is in its seventh printing. It's your highest sale yet. And now you've got your movie."

"It's not *my* movie. I want no credit for that dumb film."

"But it's based on your book. And it's very large right now. *Kill Me Tender* is cleaning up. So you can *kvetch* all the way to the bank."

"Look, I'm not complaining," I said. "I've done well financially, I'm not denying it. It's just that . . ." I hesitated, then said it quietly. "I'm having a crisis of artistic identity."

Norman briefly made a face, as if I had passed some

foul-smelling thing under his nostrils. Then he composed his expression and asked, "Okay, what's the problem?"

As I paused, wondering how best to express it, I focused for a few moments on the group at the next table. Something was going on there, and I could no longer completely ignore it.

The girl with the geometric hairdo had remained on the periphery of my vision. But I had been so caught up in my own concerns, in trying to break through to Norman, that I had paid no real attention to the agitated way she had lit the last cigarette in a package or to the stress she had conveyed when she had gone on clutching the empty matchbook between two bent fingers.

These were details that no reasonably aware novelist, no matter how self-absorbed, could fail to pick up on, and, belatedly, they registered on me. I looked at the young woman directly now and studied her as she touched up her eyebrows with an eyebrow pencil, holding a compact mirror before her as she did so.

There was something peculiar happening, all right. It was past the usual lunchtime and the dining room had pretty well emptied. But the woman and her companions remained, even though they didn't seem to be conversing in the usual sense. The fat, balding man in the blue suit may have said nothing at all; he was just a stolid, unmoving presence. The slender, gray-haired man with the maroon cravat knotted at his throat was the only one who was now speaking. But it wasn't continuous talk; he would lean forward, say something in a low voice to the woman, wait as he studied her reaction, then say something further. In all the time I had watched them, the two men had never looked at each other. Just at the woman.

"So, what is it, Hank?" Norman asked again. "What's bothering you?"

"Well, you know," I said, returning my thoughts to the matter at hand, "I, personally, am not a brutal guy. I mean, I'm not a primitive-type private eye who's never opened a book and whose only interest is in booze and broads."

"That's true," Norman agreed. "Whoever said you were?"

"Nobody. What I'm trying to say is I'm finding it hard spending my life inside Biff Deegan's head. It's very confining in there."

"And this Amos Frisby would give you more room?"

"Yes, of course. He's a classics professor at Columbia, an authority on the Hellenistic poets. That wasn't *my* academic field, exactly, but I do have an M.A. in art history from Cornell. So Amos Frisby and I have a lot in common."

"Including wit and style," Norman said with what may have been a touch of dryness.

"Yes—and elegance. I mean, Amos Frisby has elegance," I amended, "not me." I had told him the story of my proposed Frisby novel, but now I judged it advisable to fill in some of the crucial character details. "He lives in a beautiful Riverside Drive town house. He drinks only the finest wines and he eats off the best china. But above all, unlike Biff Deegan, he solves every crime"—I enunciated the words slowly—"by using his intellect."

Norman nodded gravely. "The little gray cells."

"That's right, like Hercule Poirot, and Sherlock Holmes before him, and Auguste Dupin before that. The mystery novel started off, after all, as a thinking man's form. A good detective story was a satisfying demonstration of deductive reasoning—before the troglodytes took over."

The group at the next table was leaving now. The

three of them, in single file, passed by us on their way out, the gray-haired man in the lead and the fat man in the rear, his hand lightly gripping the upper arm of the young woman, who was just ahead of him.

They swept by us quickly. But in that couple of seconds, I caught the delicate scent of an expensive perfume. And I heard the sound of something small and slight dropping onto the tablecloth beside me.

I glanced down at it. It was the matchbook the young woman had been holding.

"Okay," Norman said, "I like an ingenious puzzle as much as anyone. And if I thought this story of yours was *The Murder of Roger Ackroyd* I might feel differently—"

"I just gave you the bare outline," I said quickly. "You can't really know until I actually write the book."

"But I can tell now we might have problems with the story. I mean, the premise seems"—he hesitated, then said delicately—"precious."

"Precious?" As I waited for him to expand on this, I picked up the matchbook the young woman had discarded and nervously twisted it in my hands.

"Well, you have this Amos Frisby find a broken seashell in the pocket of the murder victim. And from that Frisby spins out a whole fancy line of reasoning that eventually leads him to the killer. Now people may have bought that kind of thing in 1890. But not today. In real life, there is rape, murder and treachery. But a broken seashell is just a broken seashell."

"To a trained mind, the smallest object has its significance," I insisted, though my confidence was faltering now. As I desperately searched my brain for some example that might help me make my point, I looked down at the empty matchbook in my hands. In the usual unthinking action of one who has picked up a discarded match-book, I opened it to confirm that there were no matches left. "It can be the—"

I didn't complete the sentence. I just stared at what was on the inside of the matchbook cover.

After a moment, Norman asked, "It can be the what?"

I was too stunned to answer. Instead, I looked quickly toward the door. But it was too late. The young woman and the two men were gone.

I gazed at the inside of the matchbook cover again, awestruck now by what had been presented to me at this all-important moment. A gift from the gods. I knew I couldn't disregard this miracle; I had to make use of it.

I closed the matchbook, looked up and said, "Norman, what if I could take something as small and ordinary as this empty matchbook and, using it as a starting point —my first clue—go out into the city and find a real-life mystery story? Would it prove my point?"

"Come on," Norman said impatiently, "let's be serious."

"I *am* being serious," I insisted. "I'm saying I can do it. If I did," I asked again, "would it prove my point?"

He looked at me in total perplexity. "It might," he said cautiously.

"And would you then let me write an Amos Frisby novel instead of doing another Biff Deegan?"

Norman's eyes focused on the matchbook in my hand. I held it up so he could see the cover. It said *Hotel Stanhope* on it, nothing else.

"What are you up to?" he asked.

"Just what I'm saying. We'll put it to the test. I maintain that any small, insignificant object, when looked at the right way, can yield a story. If I can't demonstrate it with this empty matchbook, I'll write another Biff Deegan novel."

He looked suddenly intent. "You'd write another Biff Deegan? That's a promise?"

"I promise," I said. "We'll consider it a wager between two men of honor. I'll keep my word if I lose. And you'll keep yours if I win."

He eyed the empty matchbook again, as if he was trying to figure out the catch. Slowly he said, "You'll find a real-life mystery—starting with *that* as your first clue?"

"A mystery—with intriguing, glamorous characters —and a crime behind it." I paused, then asked, "Is it a deal?"

Norman smiled now. It was the incredulous, secretly pleased smile of someone who hadn't expected to get what he wanted with such absurd ease. "All right," he said. "It's a deal."

As he turned to signal for the check, I surreptitiously opened the matchbook again to make sure that I had really seen what I had seen.

And they were there: two words written with an eyebrow pencil, almost illegible as words would be that had been scrawled blindly under a table.

Help me.

2

I left the restaurant with Norman. At the corner, I saw him off in a cab, started walking up the avenue, and then, when the cab had disappeared, turned and hurried back to Le Perigord.

There was no particular reason now for haste, of course. I had long since missed my chance to rescue the young woman—if rescue indeed was what she had needed.

Biff Deegan would have been quicker on the uptake. With his series hero's antennae, he would instantly have picked up the vibrations of a girl in distress. Or, if nothing else, he would have had the sense to realize that neat, chic ladies don't mess up other people's dining tables with used matchbooks, unless there is a reason. Biff would have glanced at the message inside the matchbook at once, rather than toying with it aimlessly, as I had done, for a minute or two. He would have pounced on the two men before they had even reached the door. Punches would have been thrown, disabling kicks would have been aimed, and a knife would have clattered to the floor as the would-be stabber screamed from the pain of a suddenly broken arm. And the girl—for one chapter, at least—would have been out of danger.

Instead, I had gone on arguing about the art of the detective novel with my editor. And so, thanks to my denseness, the cerebral path was all that was left to me, the method of inquiry and deduction. The Amos Frisby way.

When I reentered the restaurant, the maitre d' turned to me with an expression of polite concern; he assumed, probably, that I had left something behind. "Is there anything wrong, sir?"

"No, nothing's wrong," I replied. "There's just a silly little thing that's nagging at me. I wonder if you could help me."

"What is it?"

"That girl who was sitting at the table next to ours— I'm sure I know her from somewhere. But I can't place her. It's driving me nuts trying to remember."

The maitre d' gazed at the table for a moment, as if he was trying to reconstitute the group in his mind. "No, sir," he said, at length. "I don't know who she was. She was with Mr. Greville, that's all I can tell you."

"Mr. Greville?"

"Edgar Greville."

"The man with the maroon cravat?"

"Yes. He's the only one we know here. The young lady and the other gentleman were his guests."

"Did they all come in together?"

"As I remember, the young lady arrived first."

The maitre d' was a little more distant now, his tone more guarded. My questions were starting to belie my initial pretense, that I was simply trying to learn the name of an attractive young woman.

"Edgar Greville," I said thoughtfully. "I'm sure I know his name from somewhere." This was true enough; it was vaguely familiar, as if I had come across it in some trendy publication. "He's a theatrical producer, isn't he?"

"No, sir," the maitre d' said with a slight smile. "He's an art dealer."

He started to turn away, to bring an end to our conversation. Quickly I said, "Oh, yeah. He has a gallery on Fifty-seventh Street."

"He works out of his apartment, I believe," the maitre d' said over his shoulder, and then pointedly lost himself in a perusal of the list on his stand.

When I was outside again, I paused for a few moments on the sidewalk and tried to decide what to do. The girl's appeal for help had quite clearly referred to her situation with Greville and the other man. Her captors? It seemed likely. I remembered the way the fat man had kept a restraining hand on her arm when they left, as if to keep her from darting away.

I summed up as much as I now knew or could deduce. The girl had arrived first at the restaurant to keep a lunch date with Edgar Greville. The other man may have been unknown to the girl—I didn't remember her ever speaking to him—and had probably come with Greville. Who was he? Greville's bodyguard? A criminal accomplice?

At any rate, as the lunch had progressed, the situation had turned sinister, and the girl had ended up unwillingly in the custody of Greville and his associate. That would have explained why they had lingered until all the diners had left except Norman and myself. They had wanted as few witnesses as possible when they spirited the girl off into captivity.

This was fairly simple reasoning, but I felt pleased with myself nonetheless. The little gray cells were working. It didn't, however, bring me any closer to an answer to the most important question of all—where was the girl now?

Well, there was an obvious starting point for a search:

Edgar Greville's apartment. I went into a drugstore and looked up Greville in the phone book. There was a listing for him, giving an Upper East Side address that was only a few blocks away.

As I dialed the phone number, it occurred to me that Biff Deegan generally did this kind of thing differently. When he needed to find the residence of some key character, he would slap a face, bend back a finger or hang someone out of a window. But in eleven books, I had never had him do so simple a thing as look up a person in the telephone directory.

"Hello?" It was a bright, crisp, Girl Friday's voice.

"Is this Edgar Greville's residence?"

"Yes, it is."

"This is Amos Frisby." I don't know why I said it; it was just the first alias that came to mind. "Has Mr. Greville come back from lunch?"

"Amos Frisby?" she repeated uncertainly. "Does Mr. Greville know you?"

"Not yet. I'm a free-lance writer. I write on art mostly, and right now I'm doing a piece for *Art News*. I have the highest regard for Mr. Greville's expertise, and I'd appreciate it very much if he would help me out on a few points."

"Well . . . let me see. I think he just got in," she said. "Hold the line, please."

"Oh, wait a minute," I said. "My other phone is ringing. I'd better call back later. Thank you." I hung up.

Five minutes later, I arrived at Greville's building, a little breathless from the speed with which I had walked there. The apartment building was a modern high rise, and it happened to adjoin the movie theater that was showing *Kill Me Tender,* the shamelessly profitable butchery of my book of the same name.

I glanced with distaste at the poster in the display window in front of the theater. It purported to show Biff Deegan, ready for action, revolver in hand. Most of the details were accurate enough; the porkpie hat, the striped sports jacket, the .357 Magnum were as I had described them in my books. But Greg Blackwell's pretty, pouty face was a long way from being the mug of any private eye, much less my brute of a hero. The public, judging by the box office receipts, was buying him. But—to me, any-way—he came across as a slightly irritable Arthur Mur-ray's dance teacher.

Well, this was not the time to be distracted by such things. I had to concentrate, stay alert. The girl had seen me as her only hope. If I made one false step now, all might be lost.

I entered the lobby of the apartment building. A doorman was standing just inside, a pleasant-looking old fellow with a weatherworn Irish face.

"I'm supposed to meet someone here," I told him. "I wonder if you've seen her. She's young, very pretty, with dark hair, cut in sort of triangles on the sides. She's wear-ing a gray suit."

"No, haven't seen anyone like that," the doorman said. "You were going to meet her here in the lobby?"

"I think so," I replied uncertainly. "But then she might be waiting for me up in Edgar Greville's apart-ment. She was coming here with Mr. Greville."

"Mr. Greville's here," the doorman said. "But he came back alone. There was no woman with him."

"Oh. Well, I guess I should check with Mr. Greville, anyway." I started past him. "What's his apartment again?"

"Fourteen A." As I headed toward the elevator, the doorman called after me, "Your name, sir?"

"Hank Mercer." I pressed the button and watched the doorman as he unhooked his phone to announce me. But the elevator door opened immediately, and I didn't wait to find out what reception my name got.

The elevator let me out on the fourteenth floor. The door to Edgar Greville's apartment was a few steps to the right. It was the only door at that end of the hallway, which indicated a good-size apartment.

I rang the bell and the door opened instantly. I found myself confronting a uniformed armed guard from one of the private security services. "Yeah?" the guard asked coldly.

"My name is Hank Mercer. I'd like to see Mr. Greville, if I could."

"You got an appointment?"

"It's all right, Joe," a woman's voice said.

The guard stepped back, a bit grudgingly, and let me in. I was standing in a foyer now, and a youngish woman with very large pink glasses was smiling at me. I had recognized her voice as that of the Girl Friday on the phone.

"You're Mr. Mercer?" she asked.

"Yes."

"Hank Mercer, the writer?"

"Yes." I felt heartened by the possibility that I might have come across a fan. "Have you read any of my books?"

"No. But my boy friend and I saw *Kill Me Tender* last night."

"Oh? How'd you like it?"

"We loved it." With fervor, she added, "I think Greg Blackwell is divine."

"Isn't he, though?" I managed to say.

I was speaking in a higher pitch, as a precaution against the woman's recognizing my voice from my phone call, and I noticed that the armed guard was eyeing me with faint disgust.

I smiled nervously at him, then, glancing around at the paintings that lined the walls of the foyer, I said, "I assume Joe is guarding the works of art."

"Yes, but just temporarily," the Girl Friday said. "We don't usually have a guard."

That made sense. The canvases I was seeing were not items that would tempt a big-league art thief—some salon pieces by lesser nineteenth-century painters and a few unexceptional contemporary abstract works.

"He's here because of our new acquisition," she went on. "It's very valuable."

"What's your new acquisition?"

"I'm not free to tell you," she replied in a more guarded tone. She paused for a moment, then inquired politely, "What can we do for you, Mr. Mercer?"

"I'd like to talk with Mr. Greville," I said. "About a project that might be rewarding for both of us."

"What kind of project?" she asked.

"I'd rather discuss that with Mr. Greville."

"Did you write first? Or phone?"

"No, this is a sudden idea I've had. And I couldn't wait to go through the formalities. That's the way I am," I said with a smile. "Impulsive."

It was a brazen approach to take, but she returned my smile pleasantly—more pleasantly, certainly, than she would have had I not been the man who created the story of the movie she had seen the night before.

"I'll see if Mr. Greville is free," she said and disappeared through the archway.

As I waited, I pretended to study the paintings and went over the situation in my mind. If nothing else, I could feel certain that the girl with the geometric hairdo wasn't being detained in this apartment. The doorman had vouched for the fact that Greville had returned alone. And Joe, the guard, whatever his charmlessness, struck me as an honest sort, and the Girl Friday, too, seemed perfectly straight. I got no sense at all from them that they were presently involved in a kidnapping.

Greville's accomplice, then, the fat man, had taken the girl off somewhere. I would have to work on that problem later.

The woman returned. "Mr. Greville will see you now."

I followed her into a large living room. Paintings covered every bit of wall space in this room, too, and small pieces of sculpture adorned the surfaces.

Edgar Greville, looking as I had last seen him, maroon cravat and all, came toward me, his hand outstretched. "Ah, Mr. Mercer! It's a pleasure—"

The handshake was never consummated. He stopped suddenly, his face clouding over, and peered at me intently. "You were at the restaurant, weren't you?"

"Yes, I was at the next table, having lunch with my editor. It was perfect timing, I thought," I said brightly, "seeing *you* just when I was discussing my new book proposal."

"You know me?"

"Norman, my editor, knows you from somewhere. He told me who you were."

"And why was it such good timing?" Greville asked carefully.

I noticed that he had a slight foreign accent, more of a flavor than anything else. It was too faint to be able to distinguish his origin.

"Well, my new book is going to be about an art dealer," I said. "And I'd like it to be as authentic as possible. I thought it might be a good idea if I did it as a collaboration, with someone with an intimate knowledge of the art market, the art world. Like yourself. By the way," I asked, "are you familiar with my work?"

"No," he replied. "But Ruth tells me you're a well-known writer of mystery novels. And that the movie next door is based on one of your books."

"That's right."

"I suppose you make something when you sell a book to the movies," he said thoughtfully.

"A bundle. And *our* book could be a *very* big movie sale."

He smiled to himself, as if he were amused by the obviousness of my approach. Still, I seemed to have touched some vein of cupidity in him, because after a moment, he inquired casually, "Would we split it fifty-fifty?"

If this had been a real deal, I would have laughed in his face. But it was only a ruse, after all, and I could afford to nod and say, "Yes, fifty-fifty."

Greville went on smiling as he considered the prospect of megabucks. Then his expression changed to a look of cool-eyed shrewdness. "Of course, I've had offers before," he said.

I doubted it; but I knew that he was too much the negotiator to let me land him so easily. "I'm sure you have," I replied.

"My knowledge is much in demand," he went on. "Why, just a little while ago, a writer called here who wants to do a piece on me in *Art News.* Perhaps you know him? Amos Frisby?"

I was startled for a moment. "Yes, I do know him," I said. "Good writer."

Greville nodded complacently, as if he was as aware as I was of Frisby's gifts.

"Still," he said, "your proposition intrigues me. This is a work of fiction you have in mind?"

"A mystery novel. But very literate, very high class."

"Yes, that appeals to the romantic in me. All right, Mr. Mercer, I'm not promising anything. But there's no harm in talking. What kind of thing do you need to know?"

"Basically, how an art dealer operates. Let's say that my protagonist—*our* protagonist—is an art dealer who works out of his apartment, the way you do. Now," I asked, glancing around at the artwork in the living room, which was about on a level with what I had seen in the foyer, "is everything here for sale?"

"Of course," he said. "I'm not a collector. I'm in business."

"Yeah, well," I said with a touch of dissatisfaction, "that may be too mundane. Everyday buying and selling, I mean. For the purposes of our story, we'll need one big, glamorous deal. Some very valuable work of art that's at stake—with maybe a mysterious background to it. Do you ever get involved with anything really exciting?"

"In the past," he answered vaguely. "On occasion."

I wasn't about to settle for that. His Girl Friday, Ruth, had referred to a very valuable "new acquisition." And Joe, the hired security guard, had had the hard-eyed, ready-to-go-for-his-gun look of someone watching over the Hope diamond.

"But do you have anything going now?" I asked. "Something that might make a good story?"

Greville shrugged noncommittally. It was clear he didn't want to answer this question.

Ruth appeared. "Mrs. Hoskins is here," she said to her boss. "And she says she doesn't have much time."

"Oh," Greville said thoughtfully. From his look of businesslike concern, I gathered Mrs. Hoskins was an important customer. "All right. Tell her I'll be with her in a minute."

"*I* can wait," I said quickly. I drifted toward the other end of the living room. "I'll just take in your art," I said over my shoulder.

Greville didn't object—or at least, he didn't try to throw me out. So I concentrated on a marble Cupid, a turn-of-the-century American example of sentimental *dreck*.

Behind me, I heard Mrs. Hoskins make her entrance. I could hardly have missed it; she had a high-volume Texas contralto, and she was talking from the moment she came into the room. Glancing back, I saw that Greville was giving her the full, corny, continental welcome, hand-kissing and all. Soon they were standing in front of a colorful Parisian daub—something that looked like a Utrillo and wasn't—and Greville, or so I assumed, was breaking down the last of Mrs. Hoskins's sales resistance.

I was standing only a few feet away from the open doorway to Greville's office. Ruth had left the living room again, and Greville's attention was totally on his customer. I seized the opportunity and entered his office.

It was functional, modern and devoid of adornment. What I was looking for was clearly not in there. But I saw that a closed door led to another room, beyond the office.

I went over to the door, opened it and peered in. It was a small room that was almost bare, except for a bronze statue that stood on a wooden pedestal in the center. I entered, approached the statue and looked at it more closely.

It was the figure of a naked adolescent boy, caught in the midst of some graceful movement. One leg was straight and the other was flexed, with the foot on tiptoe. Both arms were extended to the sides, the right arm bent so that the hand pointed upward, the left arm bent so that the hand pointed downward. The little penis was erect. The boy's face, with its almond-shape eyes and short, broad nose, was faintly exotic, but the serene, archaic smile gave it an appealing expression. The statue was just short of life-size, about four and a half feet high; the metal seemed very ancient.

"Does it catch your fancy, Mr. Mercer?"

I turned quickly. Edgar Greville was standing in the doorway. His expression was professionally polite, but it barely concealed his anger.

"Yes, it's marvelous," I said.

"I'm glad you like it," he said. "Do you often prowl around where you don't belong?"

"Rarely. But I was curious. Your assistant told me that you had a valuable new acquisition."

His face darkened. "She did? That was indiscreet of her."

"Maybe." I gave him my most disarming smile. "But now I'm here. So can you tell me what this is?"

Greville thought for a moment. "There's no reason I shouldn't, I suppose," he said. "It's a little premature, but the press will learn about it soon enough, anyway." He came into the room and stood beside me before the statue. "This is *The Etruscan Dancer.*"

"Etruscan?"

"Yes. You know about the Etruscans, of course—that mysterious people who lived in central Italy in ancient times, whose language we can't decipher, whose history we barely know, who survive only in their works of art. This statue dates from 500 B.C.," he went on. "Aside from its beauty, it also has great value because of the rarity of its type and size. The bronze statues we have from that period are almost all quite small, figurines that are usually around a foot and a half high. This came out of the ground quite recently and was a remarkable discovery indeed."

"Who does it belong to?" I asked.

"Me," Greville answered with a little smile, "for the time being."

"How did you get it?"

"That's a long, involved story. Some of the details I'm not free to divulge. Other details I don't even know. It went through many hands before it reached me. It was smuggled out of Italy by the individuals who dug it up, was in the possession of a rather shady dealer in the Middle East, and then was sold to me. It will find its final resting place in the Metropolitan Museum."

"You're closing a deal with them?"

"At any moment now. The Metropolitan's experts have completed all their tests on this piece. *The Etruscan Dancer* is now totally authenticated."

"And how much will they pay you for it?"

"In the vicinity of two million dollars."

"Wow!" I said in an impressed tone. With a laugh, I added, "Then I guess you don't really need to do a book with me."

"Oh, one always likes to make extra money," Greville said. "Anyway, I'm only clearing a portion of the purchase price. I and my financial partners had to raise a considerable amount of capital to obtain this statue. However, my percentage is nice. *Very* nice. Now," he asked with a pleasant smile, "may I fix you a drink while we discuss this book we might be doing?"

We had switched roles, I sensed. He was now stringing *me* along, keeping the pretext alive as he tried to figure out if I had any other game than the one I seemed to be playing.

"Yes, thank you," I replied.

As we walked back to the living room, I said, "This

deal—*The Etruscan Dancer*—now that's the kind of story we can build our book around."

"If you think so," he murmured.

"I sure picked the right art dealer," I went on brightly. "But I sensed you were a blue-chip operator—that you had that aura of glamour I was looking for. I guessed it when I saw you having lunch with such a beautiful girl."

"Marisa?" His tone couldn't have been more casual. "Yes, she *is* lovely, isn't she?"

We reentered the living room. Mrs. Hoskins was gone, and we were alone again. Greville went directly to the bar. "What will you have, Mr. Mercer?"

"A light Scotch and soda, please."

"All right," he said, "if I have soda." He bent down and searched behind the bar.

"This Marisa . . ." I began.

He didn't look up. "Yes? What about her?"

"I was wondering if I'd seen her before. What's her full name?"

"Marisa Winfield." Greville, having found a small split of soda, straightened up and reached for a bottle of Scotch. "I doubt you've seen her. She's been living abroad."

"Where?"

"In Rome."

"She's just visiting here?"

"Yes. Just visiting." Greville had stopped what he was doing and, holding the bottles in his hands, was gazing at me steadily.

"Does she work with you or is she simply a friend?"

"The wife of a friend. Her husband was very dear to me. A gifted young sculptor and an outstanding art expert."

"Was?"

"He was killed recently. In a car crash."

"Here or in Italy?"

"In Italy. Near Portofino."

Greville's eyes held on me thoughtfully. He had his answer now, I suspected; he understood why I was there. He put down both bottles and said, "I don't think we'll have time for this drink after all. I have business to attend to."

There was no mistaking the sudden chill in the air. Or, for that matter, the sense of menace.

"Oh, sure," I said quickly, "I don't want to detain you. We can talk about our book later."

"Yes," he said, with an icy smile. "Some other time."

Our conversation was clearly at an end, and I got out of there as fast as, gracefully, I could.

3

My next stop was the Hotel Stanhope. Marisa Winfield had written her desperate message to me inside a Stanhope matchbook. It was reasonable to assume that she had been staying at that hotel.

I didn't really expect to find her there, though among the various possible scenarios, there seemed as much a chance of it as anything else. The fat man, for instance, might have brought her back to her hotel to gather her things together before he took her off elsewhere. Or he might be holding her semicaptive in her own hotel room.

Or, I had to face it, there might be nothing at all happening, nothing as melodramatic, at least, as the things I had imagined. Marisa Winfield, in fact, might be going on with her normal life, and her appeal for help might have referred to something else entirely, some psychological state she was in, perhaps. Or it might even have been a prank. In which case, this Winfield woman owed me an explanation.

When the cab dropped me off at the door of the Stanhope, I was struck by the appropriateness of the elegant little hotel's location. It was situated directly across the street from the entrance of the Metropolitan Museum of Art, the destined owner of *The Etruscan Dancer.*

I entered the lobby, which was quite a small area, with Early American paintings on the walls and overhanging crystal chandeliers. The reception desk was adjacent to an open doorway that led into a cocktail lounge.

I went up to the desk. A young man in a dark suit, with a curly-headed preppie look to him, was the clerk on duty. "Excuse me," I asked him, "is Marisa Winfield staying here?"

"Winfield?" The desk clerk's answer was prompt. "Yes, she is."

"Would you ring her room to see if she's in?"

"Certainly," he said, reaching for the phone on the wall at the side of the desk. "I'm pretty sure she's here. She came in just a little while ago."

"Wait a minute," I said quickly, raising my hand to stop him. "Was she alone?"

He seemed a little taken aback by the intensity in my voice. "Yes, she was alone."

"Are you sure?"

"Of course I'm sure. I talked with her. She gave me a message to leave with the switchboard."

I was already starting to feel depressed. It looked like I was in for a big letdown. "Okay, call her," I said.

As I waited for the desk clerk to get through to the room, I tasted the bitterness of my disappointment. The way it was shaping up now, I was coming out on the short end of my deal with Norman Wagstaff. Amos Frisby would be still-born and I would have to crank out yet another Biff Deegan novel.

Which meant I was doomed. I would never have peace of mind again. I would never be free.

I caught a glimpse of something very familiar out of the corner of my eye. I turned my head, looked into the cocktail lounge, and saw, with no great surprise, the big, bulky figure sitting at the bar. His face was turned away, but the porkpie hat, the striped sports jacket were unmistakable.

"She's not answering," the desk clerk said. "I don't understand."

"Oh?" I perked up a bit. "Where could she be?"

"Maybe visiting in some other room. I know she hasn't come back down."

"What was the message she left for the switchboard?"

He seemed taken aback by the blunt nosiness of my question. "I don't know if I—"

"It's not confidential, is it?" I asked.

"No," he admitted. "It's just a phone number where she can be reached when she isn't here."

"May I have that number? I might want to call her later."

The desk clerk hesitated a moment longer. But then he said, "All right," and went through the doorway behind him into the office.

I noticed that there was a paperback resting on a stool in a corner behind the desk, a thriller by my friend and competitor Wyndham Grew. It was one of Windy's lesser-known efforts, a hard-to-get title, which indicated that the owner of this copy might be a mystery buff.

The desk clerk returned, but I could see he was having second thoughts. Instead of giving the number to me, he asked, "Are you a friend of Mrs. Winfield?"

"In a manner of speaking," I said casually. "By the way, is that your book?" I asked, pointing at the paperback on the stool.

"Yes."

"Are you enjoying it? The author is a friend of mine."

The young desk clerk's eyes widened. "You know Wyndham Grew?"

"Sure. You see, I write mystery novels myself."

"What's your name?" he asked eagerly.

"Hank Mercer."

For a moment, I thought the kid might pass out. "Hank Mercer! You write Biff Deegan! Biff Deegan is my very favorite!"

"Well, I'm glad to hear that."

I couldn't help glancing into the cocktail lounge again. There was no one sitting at the bar now.

"The Bloodnight Express is the one I like the best." The desk clerk was babbling excitedly. His fannish enthusiasm was unleashed, and there was no stopping him. "You remember that scene where Biff Deegan catches the Mafia creep? The one he suspects tortured the old lady to death? And Biff puts a bullet into his gun, twirls the chamber, holds the gun to the guy's head and gives him a choice between confessing into a tape recorder or letting him pull the trigger?"

"Sure, I remember it. I wrote it."

"And the guy says, 'Pull the trigger,' and after his brains are blown out, Biff thinks, 'The verdict is in. Guilty as charged.' That was neat!"

"Yeah, I'm kind of proud of that scene," I said. "May I have that number?"

"Oh, sure," he said, handing me the slip of paper.

I glanced at it. The phone number wasn't a local one; it had a Suffolk County prefix. I transferred it to my notebook.

I put my notebook away and asked, "What's your name?"

"Jake," he replied. "Jake Hyland."

"I'll let you in on a secret, Jake," I said, dropping my voice. "I'm here on a case."

"You are?" he whispered back. He looked both ways quickly to make sure we weren't being overheard.

"Marisa Winfield is in serious danger. It may already be too late to help her. I don't like the fact she's not answering her phone."

Jake stared at me. "What should we do?"

"Let's get up to her room right away."

Jake took a key from a box and came out from behind the desk. He paused just long enough to tell the bell captain to tend to the desk for him, then headed for the elevator. He pressed the button, the doors opened and we stepped in together.

As we ascended, Jake said worriedly, "It would be terrible if anything happened *here*. This hotel has a good name."

"Violence can happen anywhere, Jake."

"Don't I know it!" he murmured fervently. Then he gave me a sidelong look and said, "You know, Mr. Mercer, *I'm* trying my hand at a mystery novel. I only have the first couple of chapters written, but I think it's pretty good."

I wasn't too startled that he was bringing it up at this moment. It has been my observation that every mystery buff has a book of his own in the works. And you can be anywhere, even in an airliner that is plunging nose-first to the earth, and he will try to force it on you.

"I'd appreciate it very much," he went on, "if you'd read it and tell me—"

"Later, Jake," I said as the elevator stopped and the doors opened.

We came out on the third floor. I followed Jake down the hall to Room 306. He had the key poised, but first he discreetly knocked on the door. When there was no response, he exchanged an anxious look with me, then unlocked the door and pushed it open.

I was half-expecting some grisly, bloody scene. But, in fact, what we saw was a perfectly ordinary hotel room, empty, but with the delicate disorder of a woman occupant in evidence. A pair of high-heel shoes were in the center of the floor. A gray jacket and skirt—the outfit I remembered Marisa Winfield wearing at lunch—had been flung carelessly onto the bed.

"Where do you think she is?" Jake asked.

"Is there any way out of this building except through the lobby?"

"Just the service entrance."

I looked at the bathroom door, which was closed. "I think we'd better check the bathroom," I said in a low voice.

There was dawning horror on Jake's face. "You think—"

"I don't know. Let's see."

We approached the bathroom door cautiously. I was about to reach out to turn the knob when the door flew open.

A woman in a bathrobe, holding a damp towel, her dark triangles of hair limp with moisture, started out of the bathroom, then froze at the sight of us. She let out a little scream of fright.

Jake was flustered. "Oh, I'm so sorry, Mrs. Winfield! We didn't know you were here."

"And what the hell are *you* doing here?" she asked in a shrill, edgy voice.

"We thought something had happened to you," Jake said. "You didn't answer your phone."

"I was taking a bath. All right? Now get out of my room!"

Jake gave me a quick, accusing look, then started retreating toward the door, drawing me back along with him. "Yes, of course," he said. "Please, forgive us. It was a misunderstanding."

I, for my part, said nothing at all. As I backed away, I just stared in wonderment at the woman with the geometric hairdo, glaring at us angrily from the bathroom doorway.

She wasn't the woman I had seen at the restaurant. She wasn't Marisa Winfield.

4

It was after dark when I got home. It had been a long, strange afternoon, and a lot of things had been thrown at me. But, as I climbed the front steps of the brownstone, I held on to just two images in my mind—almost mirror images, but not quite—the face of Marisa Winfield as I had seen it at the restaurant, and the face of the young woman in the hotel room.

I could have been mistaken, of course; they might not really have been two different persons. I was only too aware that I was capable of imagining things. And if the woman in the hotel room was an imposter, she certainly bore a striking likeness to the real Marisa Winfield—a good enough one, anyway, to fool hotel employees who had had only a few casual glimpses of the person registered under that name.

But I was sure I was right. I was good at faces. And the face of the girl at Le Perigord had haunted me all that afternoon. I could remember every detail of it.

I entered the house and walked down the hall to the door of my apartment. I had let the old newspapers pile too high outside my door and the top ones had spilled over, so that I had to kick them aside now. I felt a little guilty at this reminder of my habitual untidiness. Here I was, with the money at last to live in an elegant floor-through, an entire parlor floor on West Eleventh Street, and I was as awash in old newspapers as I had been in my cold-water flat.

I let myself into my apartment. The door opened directly into my long, high-ceilinged living room, and even though it was dark enough in it that little could be seen, I was careful not to glance around. Not yet.

I didn't turn on the light but instead crossed to the desk at the opposite wall, took off my jacket and hung it over the straight-back chair.

I waited. I sensed he was there, all right. Well, I couldn't put it off any longer. I took a deep breath, switched on a lamp and turned.

Biff Deegan was sitting in my best armchair, his pork-pie hat in place on his head.

"Was that you at the Stanhope?" I asked him.

"Who else?" Biff replied.

"Then I guess you know what happened?"

"If you know it, buddy," he said, "I know it."

"They substituted someone else for Marisa Winfield. Same size, same kind of face, same hairdo, same clothes —but some other person. Why do you suppose they did that?"

"Why are you asking me? I'm just a moron. Why don't you ask that fairy Amos Frisby?"

If Biff was going to get ugly, I didn't want to talk with him. I left the living room and went into the kitchen to heat myself a cup of coffee.

I turned on the flame under the pot. Then I realized I was hungry—I had barely touched my food at lunch— and I opened the refrigerator to select a yogurt. That was about all there was in the refrigerator—yogurt, a dozen containers of it. Also a couple of bricks of cheddar cheese, a jar of olives, a carton of eggs, fodder for my fitful snacking. I ate out frequently, of course, so I wasn't starving. But I hadn't had a well-balanced meal at home since the time of my brief marriage.

Betty Ann had been the ideal attentive wife. She had fixed me three meals a day, had tidied up after me and had made sure I was always wearing clean clothes. What she hadn't been was an Early Christian saint. She had had no resources of humility to sustain her through those long hours—almost all my waking hours, in fact—when, lost in doing my work or thinking about it, I was unaware she existed. Betty Ann had given it a good try, though, and I wished her well, wherever she was, with her new husband, whoever he was.

I was a year past forty now, with no steady girl friend. It looked like I was destined to be a permanent slovenly, ill-fed bachelor. Well, fortunately, I loved yogurt. I took out a container of strawberry, my favorite. I poured a cup of coffee, sat at the table and started spooning out the cool, creamy stuff.

I looked up. Biff Deegan was leaning against the side of the doorway, watching me.

I was distressed by how substantial he had become. When he had first started appearing to me, he had been somewhat evanescent, like ghosts in old movies. I could almost see through him. But now he seemed to be every ounce of his two hundred and ten pounds. I felt sure there must be an impression left in the armchair in which he had been sitting.

I tried to ignore him and went back to eating my yogurt. But then I heard a squeaking noise, the kind of squeak that puts your teeth on edge. It was Biff sucking on his molars. He had started doing it in one of the early books. It had seemed an effective character touch at the time, but now the sound of it bugged the hell out of me.

I looked up at him again. "Must you watch while I eat?"

"Thought you might need company," Biff said.

"I need *your* company like I need a hole in the head."

Biff shrugged and then disappeared. I don't mean that he turned and walked away. He disappeared.

As I finished the yogurt, I wondered why Biff was still so confident, so cocky. I had made quite a bit of progress that day. He had reason to worry now.

Not that I wanted to hurt him. For instance, I wouldn't have gone as far as Conan Doyle, who had tried to get rid of Sherlock Holmes by having him flung off the Reichenbach Falls. I wished Biff no harm at all. I just wanted him to get lost.

I rose and returned to the living room.

Biff was back in the armchair, but now he had his .357 Magnum out. He had broken it open and he was checking the chambers and the barrel.

I gazed at him distastefully for a moment. He was somehow managing to look even more of a slob than I had imagined. He had on the sports jacket he always wore, a brown tweed with red-striped squares, but it was as rumpled and greasy as if it hadn't been to the cleaners in a year. He was wearing one of his open-collar pink shirts; I had established that he was partial to them. But I hadn't written the two small gravy stains on the front of the shirt. He had picked those up on his own.

"I was pretty sharp today," I told him.

He glanced up at me skeptically. "Yeah?"

"Particularly with Edgar Greville," I said. "I learned what I needed to know from him. But I kept the whole thing very civilized. I was on top of the situation. Cool, suave—"

"A fucking Cary Grant, huh?"

"I displayed finesse, which is something that's totally beyond *you*, Biff. I got what I wanted by cleverness, through being subtle. By using my intellect."

"Okay," he said with his gap-toothed, taunting smile, "if you're such a brain, tell me where the girl is?"

"I don't know yet. But I've got a clue." I went to my jacket and took out my notebook, which was folded open to the phone number I had taken down at the Stanhope. "This phone number. It may lead me to the girl."

Biff was looking uninterested. He started boredly putting the bullets back into his revolver.

"The substitute gave the switchboard this number," I went on. "That must mean that Marisa Winfield was expecting to hear from somebody. And the people who abducted her don't want that person to know that anything has gone wrong. Also, they may want to get that call themselves. So the substitute won't answer the phone, and the switchboard will refer the person to this other number."

Biff had finished putting the bullets back and he now joined the two halves of the revolver.

"That's known as a deduction, Biff," I said.

"Big deal," he said.

He aimed the revolver at me, sighting along the barrel.

"Don't point that thing at me!" I snapped.

"What are you worried about? I'm a hallucination."

"I don't care. I just don't like to have guns aimed at me."

Biff chuckled and dropped the barrel a bit so that the revolver was trained on my groin. "Bang," he said.

I had had enough of his horsing around. "Look," I said threateningly, "I don't have to be such a nice guy about you. I can still throw you off the Reichenbach Falls."

He lowered his gun. "Where the fuck's the Reichenbach Falls?"

"In the Bronx, dummy. Now do me a favor and disappear. I've got a call to make."

Biff was gone, with a suddenness that almost startled me. But Dr. Ridley, my shrink, had told me that could happen, that whenever I felt strongly enough about it I could will Biff out of existence.

The only problem was, he kept coming back.

I went to the desk, picked up the phone and dialed the number in my notebook. I knew it was somewhere on Long Island, but that was all I knew. I would have to try to locate it more precisely.

There were four rings and then a man's voice answered. "Seaview Inn."

I thought quickly. A hotel? A restaurant. "I would like to make a reservation," I said.

"We're not open," he replied. "Not until Memorial Day."

A hotel or guest house, I figured. "But can't I reserve a room now?"

"The lady in charge of reservations isn't here."

"When *will* she be there?"

"Next week."

"Then what are *you* doing there?"

There was a brief pause, and then the man answered, "I'm helping with the renovations."

He sounded like he might be about to hang up, so I said quickly, "All right, then, I won't call, I'll write instead. Just give me the exact address."

He did so, providing the information I needed—the township, the road, the number. "Thank you," I said and hung up.

When I turned, Biff was there again, standing now,

gazing at me with a touch of worry in his blood-rimmed eyes. "You going out there?" he asked.

"Sure," I replied. "We'll see what we will see."

"You're out of your fucking mind," he said. "You could get blown away."

"What do you care?"

"Whaddyamean what do I care? What would happen to *me*?"

"Either way, you're finished, old man," I said genially. "Amos Frisby is taking your place."

"That's what *you* think, asshole."

He was keeping up a brave front, but I could sense that he was a little less secure in his tough-guy manner.

"Well, look at what I've accomplished," I said. "I've already won my bet with Norman. Edgar Greville—*The Etruscan Dancer*—the substitute girl at the Stanhope— and now this inn out in the country—it all adds up to a real-life mystery story. The first three or four chapters of one, anyway. So now I can write my Amos Frisby books. And *you'll* go into the big machine."

"What big machine?" he asked uneasily.

"Oh, don't you know?" I was starting to enjoy his discomfiture. "There's a big machine up in New England. It grinds all the leftover paperbacks into pulp. And then the pulp gets recycled. Think about *that*, Biff baby," I said with relish. "You're going to end up as rolls of toilet paper."

For the first time, I saw a fleeting expression of fear pass across his craggy features.

"Let's talk about this, Hank," he said with a suddenly amiable smile.

"Let's not," I said. I hated it when Biff tried to be ingratiating.

"Okay, so maybe you're a little depressed. The problem is we're in a rut," he went on reasonably. "We never go anywhere. We never get off this fucking island. Now, if we could go look for some action in some sunny place —down in the Keys, or the Bahamas—"

"I don't want to go *anywhere* with you. It's ended, Biff."

There was real incomprehension in his eyes. "Why?"

"Because I don't want to see you anymore," I said intensely. "I want to be sane again!"

Biff just looked at me and shook his head. "You spend too much time alone," he said, and disappeared.

5

arly the next morning, I got my car out of the garage and drove out to Long Island. The east-bound traffic was light, and in an hour and a half, I arrived at the Seaview Inn.

It was in one of those townships that existed for me only as signs along the Expressway on the way to the Hamptons. And the Seaview Inn itself seemed to be part of no settlement at all. It was on a dirt road that ran along the beach. The land at that spot was scrubby and the bushes went down to the sand dunes. The white, clap-board building was alone on the road.

Stone walls surrounded the property, and the front wall had an entrance gate at its center. I parked my car by the gate.

I got out and glanced around. There was nobody in sight. I turned away from the gate and looked up and down the road. I saw no other parked car.

When I turned back to the gate, I stopped, momen-tarily startled. Biff Deegan was leaning against the wall by the gate, his arms folded. His posture was as casual as if he were waiting for a bus.

I tried to ignore him as I stepped past him. But as I

was about to push open the gate, I couldn't resist looking back at him over my shoulder. Biff gave me an elaborate wink, then turned his head to gaze off into the distance.

I went through the gateway and walked up the path, taking in the inn as I approached it. It might once have been a large, three-story private house, built by some rich man who had wanted seclusion by the ocean. There was a CLOSED sign by the doorway. All the windows on the upper two floors were shuttered.

I tried the front door. It was locked. I went around to the back of the building, looking for another entrance. There was a back door, but it was locked, too.

Then I saw that the window beside the back door was open a couple of inches. I debated what to do. If I knocked and someone came to the door, I would most likely be turned away. And I hadn't driven that far to be turned away.

But there didn't seem to be anyone inside the inn to respond to a knock. As I stood by the window listening, I could hear nothing except the whisper of the surf and the cry of a sea gull, flying nearby.

I raised the window and climbed in. I found myself in a rear hall that led to an open central area. I walked down the hall and came out into a two-story-high lobby. A closed door said OFFICE on it. Beyond it were the double glass doors of a dining room. The lobby smelled musty, as if it had been months since it had been properly aired.

A straight flight of stairs led up to an open, balustraded balcony that ran along the lobby wall on the second-floor level. I went up these stairs now. The carpeting on them muffled the sound of my footsteps as I ascended.

I paused at the top. To my right, a corridor led to numbered rooms. The balcony was to my left, about thirty feet long, ending at an unnumbered door.

I was about to turn right when I heard a faint, distant voice, a woman's voice, saying some brief thing in an angry tone. It sounded as if it came from behind the door at the end of the balcony.

Moving slowly and carefully, I started along the balcony toward the door. When I was halfway there, the door opened.

A man appeared in the doorway. He stopped suddenly when he saw me. He was the balding fat man I had seen in the restaurant, still wearing his dark-blue suit, but without a necktie now.

He was briefly frozen in his surprise, and for perhaps as long as two seconds, he left the door fully open behind him. I could see Marisa Winfield, sitting on a bed. She was wearing old clothes that clearly didn't belong to her; the man's work shirt and jeans seemed several sizes too large. She was looking out of the room at me, and her face, too, registered surprise, but it was a bright, almost hopeful surprise.

The fat man closed the door. "What are you doing here?" he asked.

His voice was that of the man with whom I had spoken on the phone, and I used the same excuse again —a dumb one, considering the circumstances. "I was wondering—could I reserve a room?"

It didn't work, of course. Also, there was a dawning look of recognition on the fat man's face, as if he was remembering me from the restaurant. "How did you get in here?" he asked. "Did Max let you in?"

"No, Max didn't. I just"—I decided I might as well be honest about it—"climbed in through a window."

"Well, you're going right out again, fella," the fat man said. "Move!"

The fat man made a commanding gesture but didn't

leave his position at the door. In the next second, I realized why. There was no need for the fat man to show me the way out, since at that moment, the real muscle was coming up the stairs. I heard the heavy, muffled footsteps, turned and saw a very tall, powerfully built man in a sweat shirt—Max, I assumed—ascending unhurriedly. He was a burn case; the left side of his face had the unnatural whiteness of grafted skin, and there was only a hole where his left ear should have been. But even if he hadn't had this misfortune, he would have looked fearsome.

I went to the head of the stairs, unsure as to what to do. Marisa Winfield was in the room behind me, hoping against hope that I might rescue her. But Max looked more huge and more invulnerable with each step that he mounted.

Now there were two of us standing there. Biff Deegan was at my elbow. "Wait until he reaches the next-to-last step," he said to me in a low voice. "When he's right in front of you, push him hard in the chest. Then turn around and take care of the other guy."

Max loomed before me on the next-to-last stair, so tall that he was eye to eye with me. I shot out both my hands, pushing him backward as hard as I could. He toppled like a spinning tree trunk, describing a complete somersault on his way down and landing at the bottom with a resounding thud that shook the whole building.

I turned quickly. The fat man was coming toward me. I waited until he was almost on me, wanting to time my punch exactly. When he was a yard away, I threw a straight right at the point of his chin.

However, I hadn't thrown a punch of any kind since gym class in high school, and I missed his chin—missed all of him—by a foot or more. I went flying past him, stumbling off balance, almost falling on my face. There was a shooting pain in my shoulder and I wondered if I had dislocated it.

I recovered and, clutching my shoulder, turned back. I hadn't made a very good showing for myself, and the fat man seemed amused as he advanced toward me, with no particular urgency now.

Biff appeared again. He was off to the side, by the balustrade. "Don't just stand there," he said agitatedly. "Do something!"

But I didn't know *what* to do. I was on the other side of the fat man now, and I backed toward the door of the room, trying to keep some distance between us. My impulse was to turn, open the door, join Marisa Winfield in the room, close the door again and hold it tight until help came. But that wouldn't solve our problem. What help *could* come?

I was up against the door now. The fat man neared to within a few feet of me.

"Kick him in the balls!" Biff screamed.

I swung my foot up. I made contact this time, but not dead center in his groin. My heel caught him a little to the side, on his pelvic bone.

It hurt him, though. He let out a grunt of pain and staggered back a couple of steps. There was no amused expression on his face now. Instead, he looked very angry.

He reached down into the waistband under his suit coat, came up with a black automatic and leveled it at me. "Okay, you dumb jerkoff," he snarled, "if this is the way you want it. Get down on your knees!"

I hesitated and then obediently sank to my knees. I felt very depressed, and at the same time, I was furious at the stupidity that had brought me out here for such an absurd death.

I knew there was no escape. As if to underscore that point, Max reappeared at the top of the stairway, clutching the railing, dragging his injured leg after him. He glared at me with rage.

There were just the three of us on the balcony now, Max and the fat man and myself, helplessly kneeling. Biff was gone. He would never exist again, I thought. Not that it mattered.

The fat man approached me, bringing the barrel of the automatic to within a couple of feet of my head. I averted my eyes and tried to think of the things one is supposed to think of in the last moment of life. I thought of my mother in Rochester. And, surprisingly, I thought of Betty Ann.

I sensed the upward movement of the fat man's right arm. But it was only at the last instant that I realized what he was about to do. Then the butt of the pistol came down above my left ear and knocked me out.

I came to with a splitting pain in my head and no idea of where I was. After a moment or two, the sound of the surf and the sea gulls reminded me. I opened my eyes.

I was lying on my back on the dirt road beside my car. Slowly, carefully, I rose to a sitting position. I found myself looking dazedly at Biff Deegan, who was lounging against the fender of the car.

"A lot of help *you* were!" I said bitterly.

"What did you expect me to do?" he asked with an apologetic shrug. "I'm a hallucination."

"Then you should have kept your mouth shut. Instead, you tell me to kick him in the balls! You saw what happened."

"Well, you gotta know how to do it," Biff said reasonably.

I gingerly touched the throbbing spot on my skull. "Am I hurt bad?" I asked.

Biff came over for a closer look. "Nah," he said. "There's a little blood and you'll have a big lump there. But you'll be all right."

I struggled to my feet. I automatically felt for my wallet. The right inside pocket of my jacket was empty; my wallet was gone. Had those bums robbed me, too? But then, clutching at myself, I found the wallet in the other inside pocket. I took it out. My money was still in it.

They had checked the contents of the wallet, though, I realized, gone through it and put it back in the wrong pocket. Now they knew my name, my address and the writers' unions to which I belonged. Everything.

I went to the gate and, poking my head around the edge of the wall, peeked in. I saw no one. The Seaview Inn looked exactly the same as it had when I had first seen it, closed up and uninhabited.

I returned to the car. "Okay," I said to Biff, "that's enough of this amateur detective work. I'm going to the police."

"Whaddyamean?" Biff looked distressed. "We *never* go to the police."

"This is real life, buddy," I said. "That's a real girl in there, being held against her will by a couple of real hoodlums. In real life, when you want to get help for somebody, you call the police." I started to open the car door.

"It won't do any good," Biff said. "They won't believe you."

I turned back to him. "Why wouldn't they believe me?"

He grinned. "Because you're out of your fucking gourd, that's why."

In this particular township, as it turned out, there was no army of policemen I could summon. The police head-

quarters on the main street looked like a real-estate bro-
kerage. The police chief was an amiable, apple-cheeked
sort who seemed as if he might have been more at home
arranging a summer rental for me. And, as I told him my
story in his office, I got the impression that the two town
cops who were loitering outside comprised the major part
of the force under his command.

"You say that this woman is being held prisoner at the
Seaview Inn?" the police chief said at length, as if the
point of my narrative had only then dawned on him. "By
how many men? Two?"

"Two is all I saw."

"Why?"

"Why what? Why is she being held prisoner?"

"That's right."

"I don't know why. Do I need to give you a reason?"
Actually his perplexity was understandable. I had told
him nothing of any earlier events. I had implied that
Marisa Winfield was simply a missing friend I had tracked
down to this place. "All I can do is tell you the facts."

"The only fact *I* know right now," the police chief
said, "is that you've just admitted to breaking and enter-
ing."

For an uneasy moment, I thought he might be about
to throw me into jail. It wasn't simply that I objected to
it as a thing in itself. Rather, it would waste valuable time
that would be better spent in rescuing Marisa Winfield.

"All right, we'll deal with that later," I said impatiently. "But let's get on over to the Seaview Inn,
okay?"

"Well, we can't just go barging in there," the police
chief said. On top of everything else, he had a madden-
ingly slow way of talking. This may have been in the great
tradition of rural dicks, but it meant that a perpetrator
could cross the county line before he finished a sentence.

"It's been closed up for months. We'll have to call the caretaker to let us in."

"Then call him, for Christ's sake!"

He did so, and soon we were on our way to the Seaview Inn, the chief and his two cops in two police cars and myself, in my own car, taking up the rear.

When we got there, the caretaker was waiting for us outside the gate. He was your usual handyman-gardener type, except that he had a quiet smile a good deal of the time, as if he were privately amused by something.

The caretaker let us into the inn. He remained in the lobby, while the rest of us went straight up to the room at the end of the second-floor balcony. It was empty, with no signs that anyone had been in it recently. The gathered dust seemed untouched.

I wasn't too surprised. It was as I would have written it in one of my books.

The police chief and his men—I have to give them their due—carried out as thorough a search of the building as I could have desired. The two cops went in opposite directions, one to the third floor and one to the ground floor, and I went along with the police chief as we checked room after room on the second floor. We found nothing.

When we came back down to the lobby, the caretaker was waiting for us at the foot of the stairs.

"Anyone been here at all?" the police chief asked him.

"Not since last October," the caretaker replied. "Just me."

"Who runs this place?" I asked.

"The manager? He's down in Florida."

His gaze met mine, and there was an almost imperceptible amused glint in his eyes. He was in on this, I was sure of it.

"Then who owns it?" I asked.

"Well," the caretaker drawled, "it used to belong to the Washburns—"

"Who owns it now?"

"A realty company in the city."

"What's this company's name?"

"Prince Street Enterprises."

I jotted it down in my notebook.

The two cops returned to the lobby almost simultaneously.

"Anything?" the police chief asked them.

"Nothing," one of the cops answered.

"Okay, that's it," the police chief said.

The two cops started out.

"Sorry to have put you to this trouble, Harry," the police chief said to the caretaker.

"That's all right, Ben," the caretaker replied.

The police chief walked me to the front door. "You say you write mystery stories, Mr. Mercer?"

In an unguarded moment, I had confessed to this. I should have known it would be thrown back at me. "Yes," I replied.

"Then I guess you must have a pretty active imagination, huh?"

"Maybe. But I didn't imagine this," I said, stopping and pointing to the patch of blood-clotted hair above my left ear.

The police chief peered at it for a moment. "Yeah, that looks nasty." Then he added, "You get knocked on the head like that and you can see things."

I didn't dignify this with a response. I turned from him abruptly and walked out the door.

Biff was outside, leaning against the wall by the doorway. As I passed him, he said out of the corner of his mouth, "What did I tell ya?"

6

I drove back to the city immediately. I didn't want to miss my three o'clock appointment with Dr. Ridley.

When I arrived at my apartment, I went directly into the bathroom and washed the caked blood out of my hair. Then I swabbed the swelling lump with hydrogen peroxide. After I patted my hair back in place, I almost looked my normal, unscathed self again. Which was just as well. I didn't want to have to bring up the day's adventures with my analyst. I had gone to him because of my Biff Deegan problem, and we were exploring the innermost recesses of my being, the basic sources of my neurosis. My three-times-a-week hour with him was too precious to be wasted on peripheral issues.

I had cut it close, but Dr. Ridley's office was only a few blocks away, and at one minute after three, I took my place in the armchair opposite him.

"We're making some progress, Hank," Dr. Ridley began. "We've covered your childhood pretty thoroughly. And we've discovered how the pattern was first established."

"What pattern?" I asked. It was the first time he had used that particular word.

"It's the pattern common to many imaginative, lonely children. You were an only child with rather distant parents. So, as emotional support in your isolation, you developed a kind of positive schizophrenia. You fantasized stories. You created imaginary friends."

"Well, yes, I did. But I don't see what that has to do with Biff."

Dr. Ridley peered at me questioningly. When he would do so, he would tilt his head to one side, like an owl, perhaps to make himself seem older. He was a couple of years older than I, but he was cursed with a skinny, boyish appearance. Without his thick mustache, he would have looked like a medical student. "You don't see a connection between your Biff Deegan hallucination and your childhood imaginary friends?" he asked.

"Not really. I made up my imaginary friends because I needed companionship. It comforted me to have them around. But, believe me, I don't need Biff's companionship! He's like a nightmare that keeps coming back. He turns up when I least want him."

As if on cue, Biff Deegan appeared, standing beside Dr. Ridley's chair. He looked down at my analyst and sneered. "So this is the famous shrink, huh?"

"But you can't think of him as something separate from yourself," Dr. Ridley said. "He's an—" He broke off. "Are you all right, Hank?"

I realized I was showing my shock. But I couldn't help it. Biff had never appeared in Dr. Ridley's office before; I had thought I was safe from him there. I was shaken by the sight of him now. "Yeah, sure," I answered. "I'm all right."

"He's an extension of yourself," Dr. Ridley went on. "He's not an accident. You're willing him into existence."

Biff bent over to look at the open notebook in Dr. Ridley's lap. "What's he writing?" he asked. His face was very close to Dr. Ridley's now. "Whew! Have you smelled this guy's breath?" Biff shielded his nostrils with his hand and squinted at the top page of the notebook. "I can't read this asshole's writing. I wonder if *he* can?"

Dr. Ridley had been waiting for me to speak. "Do you see it, Hank?" he prompted me.

Biff moved away to look around the office, and I felt a little freer to carry on the dialogue. "In a way, I do," I replied. "What you're saying is—he's kind of my alter ego?"

"That's it exactly."

"But, then, he represents the worst aspects of myself. Everything I don't want to be. So why would I will him into existence?"

"Why, indeed?" Dr. Ridley asked enigmatically. "Let's think about that for a moment. Biff first started appearing to you after your wife left you."

"Yes. But that was fairly coincidental, I think."

"Was it? The breakup of your marriage wasn't a traumatic experience?"

"It was upsetting, sure. I mean, Betty Ann had taken good care of me."

Biff had finished his survey of the office and now he stood to one side of us, watching and listening.

"She loved me, and I guess I loved her, too," I went on. "She was like a mother figure to me. Every writer needs a mother figure."

"This is pretty fucking boring, Hank," Biff said.

I tried to ignore him. "And she was sympathetic to my work hang-ups. Until they got too much for her, that is. But she'd been an editorial assistant at a publishing house, so, basically, she understood a writer's problems."

"Look at him!" Biff said, gesturing toward my analyst. "His eyes are glazed."

Dr. Ridley, in fact, did have a blank, bemused expression on his face. Uneasily I hurried on to my main point. "But in a funny kind of way I felt relieved when she left me."

Dr. Ridley seemed to wake up. "Ah! You felt relieved."

"Yeah. Because I didn't have to allow for her anymore. I could just be myself."

"You no longer had a mother figure around. You were free to be a bad boy. To express the cruder, more animal side of your nature. The Biff Deegan in you."

"What bullshit!" Biff said.

"You think that's why I started seeing Biff?" I asked uncertainly.

"It logically follows, doesn't it?"

"How much are you paying this fraud?" Biff asked.

"Seventy-five dollars an hour," I answered.

Dr. Ridley looked startled. "I beg your pardon?"

"Oh, I'm sorry," I said, suddenly flustered. "I just blurted that out."

"Why?" Dr. Ridley eyed me warily. "Are you feeling a certain hostility toward me, Hank?"

"No, not at all. What I mean is," I said, groping for some plausible explanation, "we're making such progress now—and seventy-five dollars seems like a real bargain. I said it in wonderment."

It was pretty weak, but Dr. Ridley seemed almost ready to accept it. He smiled.

"Still," I continued, hurriedly returning to the main issue, "I'm not sure there's an exact correlation—I mean, between Betty Ann leaving me and my first seeing Biff. Actually, it seemed to connect with something else. Something I've never told you."

His eyebrows went up. "That you've never told me? Why haven't you?"

"I was too embarrassed, I guess. Not that it was all that big a thing."

"So, tell me now."

"Well," I began, "the first time I saw Biff was when—" I broke off. It still wasn't something I could talk about comfortably.

"Go on," Dr. Ridley urged gently.

"I got a bad review," I said.

"That must happen from time to time," he said sympathetically.

"No, not to me. Because my books are paperback originals, and they don't get reviewed much at all. But some critic for a pretty big magazine decided to review one of my Biff Deegan novels. He really did a job on it. He slaughtered it."

Biff, I noticed, was gazing at me intently now, as if he was concentrating on my every word.

"I don't understand," Dr. Ridley said. "What does that have to do with your hallucination?"

"Well," I went on, "when I read the review, I was absolutely devastated. But after the first shock wore off, I suddenly thought, 'Biff will take care of that bastard. He'll shove every rotten word down that guy's throat.'"

Biff nodded grimly. There was a savage gleam in his eye.

"And then I turned around," I said, "and there he was."

"This was the first time you saw him?"

"The first time. The first time he was actually *there.*"

"Was he angry?"

"He was furious."

"What did the review say, by the way?"

"Must I repeat it?"

"Perhaps you don't remember."

"Oh, I remember, all right," I said. "It's branded on my brain." I paused, then recited, " 'Mr. Mercer expects us to take an interest in a hero who is nothing more than a sadistic Neanderthal.' "

"That son of a bitch!" Biff said through clenched teeth.

" 'In fact, Biff Deegan is a dull clod, his behavior is nauseating, and the prose that describes his antics is witless and feeble.' "

Biff had become highly agitated. He took out his .357 Magnum, brandished it wildly and roared, "I'll kill that miserable creep!"

I could no longer avoid looking at him. I just stared at him now. Dr. Ridley, a puzzled expression on his face, followed the direction of my eyes.

At length, he asked in a soft voice, "Hank, are you seeing Biff now?"

"Yes," I admitted.

"How long has he been here?"

"Almost from the beginning of the hour."

Dr. Ridley glanced about nervously, as if he thought there might be some chance he could locate my mental aberration at a point in space. Biff had calmed down, had put his revolver away, and was facing my analyst at a distance of about eight feet. But Dr. Ridley managed to look at every spot except where Biff actually was.

"Has he been talking?" Dr. Ridley asked.

"He's said a few things."

Dr. Ridley's eyes narrowed to paranoid slits. "What has he been saying about me?"

"Nothing bad," I lied.

Dr. Ridley shifted his position cautiously in his chair and faced in the general direction of Biff. "Tell me where he is."

"Right in front of you."

Biff stepped closer to Dr. Ridley, leaned forward, put his hands to his ears and wagged them, and stuck out his tongue.

Dr. Ridley extended a tentative hand. "Here?"

Biff recoiled. "Tell him if he touches me I'll break his fucking arm!" he growled.

Dr. Ridley withdrew his hand, looked down at his notebook for a moment and then closed it. He was clearly unstrung.

"I think you need a rest, Hank," he said. "We *both* need a rest. That's enough for today."

Biff was step for step with me as I walked home, but I didn't say a word to him. For one thing, I was too angry at him. Also, of course, I didn't want to give people the impression that I was talking to myself on the street.

But when I was safely inside my living room, I whirled on him and asked sharply, "Okay, what was all *that* about?"

"Whaddya mean?" Biff asked innocently. "What did I do?"

"Don't pretend you don't know! You almost undid a year of intensive therapy. I'll be lucky if Dr. Ridley lets me come back now. He may turn me over to Bellevue instead."

"You might be better off, buddy," Biff said with a short laugh.

"Don't try to be smart," I said. "You can't begin to comprehend all I've accomplished with Dr. Ridley . . . the understanding of myself I've gained."

"So, I got curious," he said with a shrug. "I wanted to see for myself."

"Well, you shouldn't have!" I burst out furiously. "You had no right being there! That's sacred territory!"

"What's so sacred about it? And why don't I have any right?" he asked, suddenly indignant. "Don't you think I've got an interest at stake—when you and that shrink are talking about me behind my back?"

"It *has* to be behind your back. You can't be there," I insisted. "It's not fair if you're there. If you're there too I'll *never* get rid of you."

His indignation vanished and now he looked sorrowful. "It doesn't make sense, Hank," he said sadly. "Why should you *want* to get rid of me?"

"Let's not go into that."

"Haven't we had some good years together? And haven't I given you all this?" With a sweeping gesture, he indicated the huge living room and its new, expensive furniture. "Haven't I made you a star?"

"I'm not the star. *You* are," I said with some bitterness.

"It's been the two of us together, buddy. And now you want to junk me!" He looked at me accusingly. "You owe me an explanation, Hank."

"There's nothing to explain. I've just outgrown you, that's all."

"Oh, no, you're not going to weasel out of it with *that* kind of answer. I'm not letting you off this time," he said, leveling his finger at me. "Tell me once and for all. Why do you want to dump me?"

I blurted it out. "Because I'm ashamed of you, that's why!"

As soon as I said it, I knew I had gone too far. Biff looked stricken. Then his lip quivered. He sank slowly into an armchair and stared at the floor. It seemed almost impossible to believe—and, since the brim of his porkpie hat blocked my view of his face, I couldn't be sure—but I thought, from the heaving of his back, that he might be crying.

I felt rotten now. Guiltily I went over to him and stood beside him.

"I'm sorry. I shouldn't have said that," I said. "You've meant a lot to me, Biff, really you have. And we've had some good times together. But everything has to come to an end."

"It hasn't been easy for me, you know," he said in a muffled voice.

"What hasn't been easy?"

"Some of the things you've made me do."

"Like what?"

"Like, some of the weird things I've had to do with women." Biff straightened up and looked at me. "That shrink is right. It's you—not me. *Your* sickness. Sometimes I wish you'd just go out and get laid instead of getting off through me."

"But you enjoy it," I insisted.

"You think so? Show me! Show me where in any of the books I enjoy it."

I couldn't be sure, but I had a feeling he was right. I was usually so caught up in describing action that I didn't go into subjective states. "Most of it is just harmless sex, anyway," I said.

"Yeah? What about the time I stuck the barrel of my gun up inside that girl? What do you call that?"

"Well—it's commercial."

"To you, it's commercial; to me, it's disgusting!" His leathery face was twisted with revulsion. "What if my mother read something like that?"

I paused, struck by the idea. It had never occurred to me, but Biff, of course, had a mother, and perhaps a family, too, somewhere. It was a possibility I hadn't explored.

Well, the books were closed on Biff. And, anyway, this wasn't the time to speculate on such matters. I remembered that I had a kidnapped girl to worry about.

"Okay," I said, "we'll talk about this later. Right now I have to figure out what to do about Marisa Winfield."

I went into the bedroom and hung up my jacket in the closet. When I came out to the living room again, Biff was gone.

I poured myself a Scotch on the rocks, then went over to the armchair that was by the tall parlor-floor windows. It was my thinking chair; I would sit in it, staring out at the street, whenever I had some thorny creative problem to work out. Now I settled into it with my drink to mull over my current dilemma—how to proceed in my search for Marisa Winfield.

It looked like I wasn't going to have any help. The police in the Long Island township weren't about to do anything; the police chief, I knew, had me pegged as a mental case. And, at any rate, the kidnappers were probably safely out of their jurisdiction. As for the people at the Stanhope, they were content that everything was in order, that Marisa Winfield was safely ensconced in her room. And without any evidence of a crime—more evidence than an empty matchbook with two scrawled words in it—I couldn't go to the New York police.

In fact, I realized now, I had no corroboration for any of this story. It wasn't simply a matter of Marisa Winfield's plight; I was no closer to solving my own plight. An author's word was worthless currency to an editor. Without some proof, I couldn't win my bet with Norman.

How could I establish proof? How could I get the New York police to verify this mystery? Someone would have to register a complaint or report Marisa Winfield as a missing person. Did she have any family, friends or business associates who would have noticed her disappearance? At that point, I didn't know, since I knew next to nothing about the woman in question. That was obviously the next step in my investigation. I would have to find out more about Marisa Winfield.

Lost in thought as I was, I had been only dimly aware of the gray sedan that was cruising slowly down the street and had now come to a stop at the curb outside the house. And so I was totally unprepared for the sudden, loud gunshot and the simultaneous shattering of the window beside me.

I reacted instantly, though. Without quite knowing how I got there, I found myself facedown on the floor. I didn't move, didn't even breathe, as I waited tensely to see if there would be any further shots.

But there was only silence now. After a moment, I sat up and looked around. Biff was by the shattered window, his gun drawn, pressed back against the wall as he peered out.

"They're gone," he said.

"Did you get a look at them?"

"No more than you saw."

Dazedly I wiped my dripping left arm; my drink had gone flying, and the whiskey had ended up partly on the carpet, partly on my arm and leg. I heard a tiny thump behind me and quickly looked around. A chunk of plaster had fallen from the ceiling, from the spot, I assumed, where the bullet had entered. I hoped it hadn't gone up through my upstairs neighbor's floor. He had been complaining, as it was, about my late-night typing.

The telephone rang.

I flinched at the ring, as if it were still another attack on me, and stayed where I was. Then, as the phone kept

ringing, I rose, went to the desk and picked up the receiver. "Hello?"

"That was a warning shot." I hadn't heard this voice
before. It was deep and rough and spoke as slowly as a
recorded announcement. "You only get one warning. The
next shot you get in the head. Don't call the cops. Don't
do anything. Just keep your nose out of other people's
business."

There was a sharp click.

I hung up and turned. Biff was right next to me,
sucking on his molars thoughtfully.

"Well, I guess that's it," he said.

Something about the smirk that came onto Biff's face
—and the maddening squeaking sound he was making—
suddenly gave me the courage of ten men. "Don't be so
sure," I said. "I'm going ahead with this. I'm going to find
Marisa Winfield."

"You looking forward to being dead?"

"I'm looking forward to winning that bet with Norman. But I'll have to be sharp," I went on. "And I can't
think clearly with you around. Leave me alone for a while,
will you? Let me handle this case alone."

"If that's the way you want it," Biff said with a shrug.
"But I'll be there if you need me." He smiled. "And you
will."

He disappeared.

7

By the time I had swept up the plaster and pieces of glass, I had decided on the next step in my investigation. I went to the phone and called my Italian translator in Rome.

I had never phoned him before, but I had his number in my book. I tried it now, and in a matter of moments, through the miracle of modern telecommunications, I was talking, over a distance of five thousand miles, with Gaetano Bruneschi.

Gaetano's voice was rather faint on the line, but he sounded delighted to hear from me. "Hank! What an astonishment! Have you received our new book?"

Kill Me Tender had just come out in the Mondadori edition, and Gaetano, as always, had done the translation. "Yeah," I replied, "my agent forwarded the copies to me last week."

"How do you like it?"

"Well, I can't say. I don't know Italian."

"I really labored over it," he said. "I gave it my best explosion."

After a perplexed moment, I realized he meant, "I gave it my best shot." Gaetano, when he spoke English, was sometimes unlucky in his choice of words. It was a characteristic that left me a little uneasy about the strict accuracy of my Italian texts.

"It *looks* beautiful, Gaetano," I said.

"I wish you could read it, Hank," he said. "I wish you could see how well I retrieve your style."

"I don't doubt it. But I'm not calling to talk about the book."

"Oh? What is it?

I imagined the hyperalert expression that had doubtless come onto Gaetano's face. I remembered that expression from the one time I had met him, when he was passing through New York and had looked me up. He had been on his way to California, where he was going to make pilgrimages to whatever was left of Raymond Chandler's Los Angeles and Dashiell Hammett's San Francisco. For one afternoon, I showed him Hank Mercer's New York.

Gaetano, a dainty little man with a bushy mustache, took in everything with the hungry curiosity of a street sparrow. And that alert look would click onto his face whenever anything promised to be at all remarkable.

I questioned him about his life in Rome, and Gaetano proved to be informative; not about himself—his own existence seemed bookish and uneventful—but about a delicious assortment of scandals involving the glittering, decadent types who made up Rome's social set. I got the impression that Gaetano was like one of those watchful Fellini extras who observe knowingly from the background of a scene but are never at the center of the action.

It had occurred to me that he might be just the man I needed now. And so in answer to his question, I said, "I could use your help. I need to find out about someone who lives in Rome."

"Who?"

"Have you ever heard of a sculptor and art expert named Winfield?"

"The name is familiar . . ." He paused, then admitted, "No, I do not know him."

"Well, he's dead now, anyway. Killed in a car crash. The person I really want to know about is his widow, Marisa Winfield."

"An old lady?"

"No, young and beautiful."

"Ah!" Gaetano said appreciatively. "What is this for, Hank?"

"I'm working out another novel," I replied. "But this time it will be based on real people."

"It will happen in Rome?" he asked with some excitement.

"A lot of it, I think."

"Wonderful! I will find out about this Marisa Winfield immediately. And then I will back up to you."

"Get back to me? Fine. Thanks, Gaetano."

My next phone call was to the Stanhope. If I had figured it out correctly, the phony Marisa Winfield, if she was still there, wouldn't answer her room phone. But there was some chance that a new alternate number had taken the place of the Seaview Inn number; an answering service, perhaps, or some other go-between kind of phone number. Not likely, perhaps, but I couldn't pass up any possibility.

As it turned out, I drew a blank. "She's checked out," the Stanhope operator told me.

"Did she leave an address or phone number?"

"No, nothing," the operator said.

I had lost the trail completely now. What could I do to pick it up again? I knew better than to go after Edgar Greville a second time. With that gunshot still ringing in my ears, it didn't seem prudent to advertise my continued interest in this case.

I could try discreetly checking out all of Greville's associates. But that would mean a prolonged dogwork investigation, and I lacked the talent for that kind of thing. It was the drab work that real-life private detectives did, not Biff Deegan and the other fictional shamuses. I only understood fiction, not everyday life. Which meant that, as in a good mystery novel, I now had to have a lightning flash of inspiration that would lead me directly to the center of the tangled web.

But no lightning flash was forthcoming, and I could only go on poking at the situation with simple reason. I analyzed it, broke it down logically and kept coming back to the same interesting point: Two women were involved, not one—Marisa Winfield and the substitute. It was just about impossible to find the real woman, but there was a chance, it occurred to me, that I might be able to find the phony.

I had already given her some thought. I knew that she was a young woman of the same general age as Marisa Winfield, and with a physical resemblance to her that had been heightened by identical makeup and clothes. I assumed she had carried out the imposture for pay. An out-of-work actress, possibly; though that deduction wasn't too helpful, since in New York City, it narrowed down the possibilities to about ten thousand women. It still left me at a loss as to how to locate her.

And then it struck me. The key was her hairdo.

That distinctive geometric hairdo, the striking pattern of inverted triangles, had been the most important part of the impersonation. It had matched Marisa Winfield's coiffure down to the last strand of hair. It was a hairdo I had seen a few times before, pictured on

women's pages and in fashion sections. I had the feeling
that it was the creation of some currently chic hairstylist.

It had undoubtedly been imitated by lesser hairdressers. But Marisa Winfield had impressed me as the kind of
classy lady who would have settled for nothing less than
the master himself. Perhaps she had made an appointment at his salon as one of her first actions upon arriving
in New York.

Then, when carrying out a conspiracy to commit so
serious a crime as kidnapping, wouldn't Edgar Greville
have taken special care? Wouldn't he have sent the substitute to that very same salon? And to achieve such an
uncanny match, wouldn't the girl have had to bring along
a current photograph of Marisa Winfield?

It was a rather wild conjecture, I knew, but it had the
feel of the golden hunch to me, the inspired guess, the
magical leap of reason that could turn a case around for
a brilliant, cerebral detective—a Hercule Poirot or a Nero
Wolfe. Or an Amos Frisby.

I was stopped by one thing, though. My knowledge
of hairstyling and hairstylists was almost nil.

Well, it was no problem. There was someone who
could help me, an expert who knew exactly who was
doing what in that particular field. I decided I would see
her the first thing in the morning.

I was up late that night, working on the drawing. I did
it over several times until I had it right.

Finally it was there on my sheet of drawing paper, as
close a likeness as I could come up with, working from
memory alone, of Marisa Winfield.

It wasn't a bad job, actually. I had once thought seriously of becoming an artist, had taken classes for a while,

and I had developed a fair amount of technical competence. Unfortunately, that had been about it. The spark hadn't been there.

But I knew I was destined to be *some* kind of artist —and the jobs I had in my early manhood made me all the more determined to find my niche as one. There may be people in this world who are cut out to be bill collectors, airline ticket agents and restaurant captains, but I clearly wasn't one of them, and I quit all these jobs, in each case, it seemed, just hours before I was about to be fired.

I gravitated more and more to the writing of fiction. I tried a few short stories in the *New Yorker* style. Then, as my first full-scale effort, I wrote a sensitive novel about my coming of age in Rochester. I labored over it for two years. I was inordinately proud of it and I was totally baffled when sixteen publishers turned it down.

As an act of cynical desperation, I wrote a mystery novel. My idea was that I might pick up a quick buck that way to subsidize my *real* writing.

I created a private-eye hero, named him Biff Deegan, and then the book just happened, in four or five weeks. I didn't have the feeling I was really writing it; rather, Biff Deegan took it away from me and was off and running, and I clung on for dear life.

This book was *Murder on Ice*—still, perhaps, my best-known title—and it was bought by the first editor to see it, Norman Wagstaff. Norman took me to an Irish bar for a cheeseburger—we didn't meet at places like Le Perigord until the later, flusher days—and our long relationship began—the intense, and sometimes uncomfortable, partnership between Norman, Biff and me.

There were no more odd jobs after that, and there was no more drawing. Which was a pity, I thought as I put the finishing touches on my portrait of Marisa Winfield. I

was rediscovering how enjoyable it could be to lose yourself in an absorbing but nonverbal act of creation.

And I hadn't lost whatever talent I had, it seemed. I
still had my knack for representational accuracy. As I
studied the portrait, I saw that I had caught most of the
details, in particular—and this was the most important
thing—the precise nuances of the geometric hairdo.

My agent never sits with his back to the door.

It's not that Perry Rose has anything to fear from the
underworld—or from enraged editors or embittered cli-
ents, for that matter. It's just his style. He has spent so
many of his waking hours reading his special kind of mer-
chandise—thrillers and hard-boiled mysteries—that it is
as if he has never quite emerged from the slush pile. He
continues to walk down perilous dark alleys, trailed by
shadowy, sinister figures who mean him no good.

Over the years, Perry has taken on the appearance of
an inhabitant of pulp thrillerdom—one of the villains, for
some reason, rather than a hero. He is a swarthy, bearded
man with a cunning cast to his features. Norman Wagstaff
once described him as looking like "the kind of guy you
expect might try to sell you the Maltese Falcon." Actually
Perry is fairly straight in his business dealings, a law-abid-
ing citizen and as considerate and loyal an agent as an
author could hope for.

But he does have his haunted vision, and he can make
an ordinary business meeting seem like a rendezvous in
Istanbul. And that morning when I turned up at his office,
there was, in fact, a certain mystery to my visit. I had told
him nothing on the phone about my reason for wanting
to come in.

So Perry went through his usual ritual. After greeting

me, he eyed my briefcase warily, as if he wondered what ominous secret papers it contained. Next he closed his office door, checking the waiting room first to make sure no one was lurking outside. Then he returned to his desk, looked thoughtfully at the window as if he was uncertain whether to draw the blinds, and sat.

"I talked to Norman," he began.

He kept his voice low, as if he didn't want to risk being overheard. Actually there was no one around who could hear our conversation, other than his new junior associate, Harriet, who was in the smaller adjoining office.

"He says you may be writing another Biff Deegan after all."

"Oh?" I was a little taken aback. Was Norman *that* confident of winning the bet?

"And, speaking for myself," Perry went on, "I'm glad to hear it. I mean, I'd never tell you what to write. But you know my philosophy—when you've got a good thing going, stick with it."

"I've been sticking with it for eleven books," I said. "Isn't it possible that that's too much of a good thing?"

Perry gave me his oily chuckle, his Sidney Greenstreet one. "Maybe. But we can't say the Biff Deegan phenomenon has peaked yet—not with the new movie about to start shooting."

"Already?" This was news to me. I was aware that to capitalize on the success of *Kill Me Tender, The Bloodnight Express* was being rushed into production. But I had been given no dates. "Where?"

"Right here in town. They'll start the location shooting this week. Greg Blackwell arrived a couple of days ago."

"How thrilling," I said.

Perry smiled to himself as he picked up on the sour

note in my voice. "He's not your favorite actor, I know," he said. "I suppose he *does* leave something to be desired as Biff."

"That's putting it mildly."

Actually my dislike for Greg Blackwell began before I ever saw him on screen playing my creation.

I had flown out to L.A.—uninvited—when *Kill Me Tender* was shooting. I had been so excited by the idea of a book of mine being made into a movie that I just couldn't keep away. The producer seemed less than happy to see me. But rudimentary courtesy required that I be introduced around.

A publicity man brought me to the star trailer to meet Greg Blackwell. This led to some initial confusion. Greg Blackwell somehow got it into his head that I was a fan magazine writer come to interview him, and he had given orders that there were to be no interviews of him while they were shooting. He told his valet to throw me out of the trailer, and the man started to do just that—by force.

When the publicity man quickly explained that I was the author of the book they were filming, Greg Blackwell said, "That makes it even worse!"

But then, after this unguarded comment, his manner changed and he was all honeyed charm with me. We had five minutes of reasonably civilized conversation.

The damage had been done, though, and I was left with that initial bad impression. It was the correct one, I was sure.

"What are they shooting first?" I asked Perry now.

"The factory sequence."

"The factory sequence? That's the end of the story."

"You know how these movie people work. Backass-wards."

"Well, they can tell the story upside down, for all I care," I said. "I disown the whole project."

"May I still cash the checks?" he inquired dryly.

"By all means. I just don't want to have to think about that movie. Or about Biff Deegan. They can have him. I'm on to other things."

Perry went expressionless. "Your new character, you mean?"

"Yeah. I hate to disappoint you, Perry, but I think Norman misinformed you. I'm going strong with Amos Frisby. Making real progress."

"That's what you've got in there?" he asked, pointing at my briefcase.

"No," I replied, unclasping the briefcase, "I've got this."

I took out the drawing of Marisa Winfield and handed it to him. He looked at it uncertainly. "Who's this?" he asked.

"Oh, just a girl," I replied vaguely.

"What am I supposed to do with a drawing?"

"Nothing," I said. "You're not the one I need to talk to. I want to talk with Harriet."

"Harriet?" he echoed, a bit perplexedly. He had taken on his new associate, Harriet, to handle women's fiction. This, obviously, wasn't my province. "Why?"

"I need her help on a technical detail in something I'm writing now. A small point of accuracy, but you know how I like all my touches to be authentic."

This wasn't particularly true at all—I could be as careless as the next writer—but Perry, loyal agent that he was, nodded dutifully.

"I remembered," I went on, "that Harriet used to be an editor on a beauty magazine."

"That's right," he said. "Up until a few months ago."

He left the rest of it unmentioned—that Harriet, after years of faithful service, had been dismissed as part of a staff cutback. Editorial jobs were harder to come by than ever, and now she was trying her hand at agenting.

"Well," I said, indicating the drawing, "I'm describing a character as having this hairstyle. I've seen it around here and there, but I don't know who created it. I thought maybe Harriet could tell me."

"All right." Perry picked up the telephone receiver and poked a button. "Harriet, would you come in here, please?"

In a minute, Harriet appeared. She was a fortyish lady, coiffed, heavily made up, in a gauzy dress. She looked like a character out of a white telephone movie who had wandered into Perry's film noir.

Perry wasted no time on explanations. He handed the drawing to Harriet and said, "We need to know something. Whose hairstyle is this?"

Harriet glanced at the drawing and answered promptly. "You can't mistake *that* look. Valerian Carew."

This happened to be one of the very few hairstylist names I recognized. "Oh, yeah, Valerian Carew," I repeated. "He's pretty big, isn't he?"

"Right now he's all the rage," Harriet said. "This is his latest style, and it's the talk of the field." She gazed at the drawing appreciatively. "It's sort of the twenty-first-century look. Too daring for most women. But it suits this girl's face."

"His salon is midtown somewhere, isn't it?" I asked.

"It's just a couple of blocks from here. Over on Madison."

8

Valerian Carew's salon was in a town house that might once have been the private residence of some dignified, turn-of-the-century merchant prince. When you went through the front door into the foyer, though, all dignity ended. It was hard sell everywhere you looked. Glass cases displayed the various Valerian Carew lines of goods: cosmetics, wigs, perfumes. The walls were covered with photographs of women celebrities—movie stars and international socialites—with written testimonials on them to Carew's art. There were so many cut flowers around that the foyer had the sweet oppressiveness of a florist's shop.

The receptionist at the desk did not encourage me in my hope of being given a moment of Carew's time. But when I persisted, stressing the urgency of my business, she allowed me to take a seat while she periodically called back to see if the great man was free.

I sat there for twenty minutes or so, surrounded by women who read magazines as they waited to be coiffed. Then I was sent back to Carew's office, which was at the rear of the main floor, at the end of a long hall. The door was open, and I went in.

Valerian Carew was standing dead center in his office, waiting for me—or, I supposed, for anyone who might happen in at that moment. He was poised impatiently on the balls of his feet, as if he had only very temporarily lighted on the spot.

"Yes? What do you want?" he asked me. "Tell me quickly, please. My next appointment is in two minutes."

He spoke with an authoritative crispness that belied the soft boyishness of his appearance and was a little incongruous, in fact. A drill sergeant's tone somehow did not go with a peppermint-striped sport shirt and bleached bangs.

Since he didn't seem to believe in the usual civilities, I wasted no time on them. I immediately took out my drawing of Marisa Winfield and showed it to him. "Do you know this woman?" I asked.

"She was in here last week," Carew replied, after taking in the drawing at a glance. There was no hesitation. He obviously had an extraordinary memory for faces.

"And you did her hair?"

He paused now. "Are you a policeman?" he asked.

"No, I'm a writer."

Interest quickened in his eyes. I hadn't said anything that specific, but to the publicity-hungry, the mere suggestion of ink can be enough.

"Which publication are you with?" he asked, more cordially.

"None of them. I write novels. Mystery novels."

His interest died. "How boring!" he said.

At that point, a thin young man in shirtsleeves burst into the office. He was quite angry. "Val," he said, "you're going to have to talk to Michael."

"About what?" Carew asked, very wearily.

"He's taking Mrs. Stewart again. And he *knows* she's my customer."

"Calm down, Rudy. I'll speak with him. But let me finish with this man first," Carew said, turning to me. "With—what's your name again?"

As it happened, he hadn't bothered to ask before. "Hank Mercer," I answered.

This, as I might have expected, registered zero on Valerian Carew. But Rudy, I noticed, suddenly looked at me with curiosity. As far as name recognition went, I was batting .500 in this office. I couldn't hope for more—not with hairdressers, anyway.

"Now, why do you want to know about this woman?" Carew asked, pointing at the drawing. "What are you after?"

"I'm not trying to find out anything about *this* woman," I said. "What I want to know is this. Did another woman come in, sometime in the last week, show you a photograph of this woman, and ask you to cut her hair in exactly the same way?"

He seemed briefly startled by the question. "What business is that of yours?"

"I'm just asking," I said, trying to keep my tone mild and my smile pleasant. "Yes or no?"

"Neither. I would never dream of answering such a question," he said indignantly. "That kind of thing is highly confidential information. I'm like a doctor or a priest. Understand? A client's secrets are safe with me. Now if you don't mind, I have to get back to work." He started toward the door.

"Mr. Carew," I blurted out dramatically, "a woman's life may be at stake!"

Valerian Carew turned back in the doorway and fixed me with his cold gaze. "How boring!" he said, and disappeared.

I was left standing there holding the drawing, and with what I guessed was a foolish expression on my face.

Rudy, who had remained in the office, smiled at me sympathetically.

I smiled back at him ruefully and, for lack of anything else to say, murmured, "Difficult, isn't he?"

Rudy shrugged. "That was nothing. You should see him when he's in a bad mood."

I started to put the drawing back into my briefcase. "May I look at that?" Rudy asked suddenly.

I turned the drawing around, showing him the pictured face. He looked at it intently for a moment but made no comment. "I'll walk out with you," he said.

We left the office. As we started up the long hall, heading back toward the front of the building, Rudy asked, "What you said—about some woman being in trouble—is that true?"

"I wasn't making it up. It's a matter of life and death. But that didn't seem to impress your boss."

"He couldn't tell you anything, anyway. He didn't cut her hair."

I stopped and stared at him. "He didn't cut *whose* hair?"

"The woman who came in with the photograph. Val didn't cut her hair. I did."

"Who is she?" I asked quickly. "What's her name?"

Perhaps I should have played it a little cooler, because Rudy, hearing the urgency in my voice, turned coy. He had a goading little boy's smile now, of the I-don't-know-if-I'm-going-to-tell-you variety.

"Well, you know," he said, "Val meant it. We're not supposed to talk about our customers." He paused. "But I could be persuaded."

"Then tell me! Please!"

I was being dense. Entreaties weren't what he wanted. "I could be persuaded," he repeated.

I got the point. I reached for my wallet and checked

what I had in it. Not much. I took out the twenty-dollar bill. Rudy looked blank. I took out another twenty dollars in smaller bills. That left me just enough to get home by subway.

Rudy seemed disappointed. But what was I supposed to do? Use my American Express card for a bribe?

Then, plucking the bills from me with his fingertips, he said, "I'll check my appointment book. Wait for me out in the foyer." He turned and went back down the hall.

I returned to the foyer and once again took my seat among the waiting women. Two minutes passed and then Rudy reappeared. He handed me a slip of paper. " 'Bye now," he said, and left.

I glanced at the name written on the slip of paper. "Carolee Denker."

When I entered my apartment, I looked around. From force of habit only. I knew Biff Deegan wouldn't be there. Not after my little triumph of deductive reasoning. He would be off sulking somewhere, counting the days until his extinction.

I had found out the substitute's identity in less than twenty-four hours. Normally, after so little time, Biff would still be careening around in car chases and banging away at people, no wiser than he was before. Whereas *I* had the girl's name in my pocket—Carolee Denker—and I hadn't even worked up a sweat. Amos Frisby himself couldn't have done better.

My shattered window had been replaced, I noticed; the super evidently had let the glazier in while I was out. The new, unsullied glass was allowing more light into the living room than I was used to. Things were looking brighter all around.

The phone rang. When I answered it, an operator

told me that I had a call from Rome, from Gaetano Bruneschi. Would I accept the charges? "Yes, put him on," I
said.

There was a pause, then I heard Gaetano's cheery
voice. "Hank, how are you?"

"Fine, Gaetano. Things are going pretty well. What
about you? Have you found out anything about the Winfields?"

"Yes, I have found out a lot. I have been like a real
private eye, Hank. You should be proud of me."

"Well, I'm appreciative. I hope you didn't have to go
to too much trouble."

"No, it was not difficult. I simply talked to a few
friends of mine who are—how do you say it?—in the
know."

"And did they know the Winfields?"

"They knew them—or knew about them. The Winfields were a very glamorous couple. They were invited to
all the best parties."

"They were rich, huh?"

"No, they had no money. But they had—you know—
la bella figura. Style. They looked nice."

"And he was a sculptor?"

"Peter Winfield? A sculptor, yes. Nothing great. Just
okay. But he was a scholar, too. An important scholar."

"Yeah, I know, an art expert. Did he have a special
area?"

"Yes. Etruscan art."

"What?"

I was a little startled. The image of *The Etruscan
Dancer,* as I had seen it in Edgar Greville's apartment,
came back to me. The sale of it to the Metropolitan was
clearly going to be the major coup of the art dealer's
career. But it hadn't occurred to me until that moment

that there might be some connection between the statue
and Marisa Winfield.

Gaetano, who may have misinterpreted my reaction
as incomprehension, explained, "The Etruscans. They
were a people in ancient times who lived north of here,
and—"

"Yes, thanks, Gaetano, I know all about that."

"Okay then," he went on. "This Peter Winfield, he
knew more about Etruscan art than anyone in the world.
In that field he was top tomato."

"Top banana? Yeah, good. Now, what about Marisa
Winfield? What did you find out about her?"

"She is a beautiful girl. That is the first thing anyone
says."

"I was aware of that already."

"Her mother is Italian and her father is American.
She grew up here in Italy but went to school in New
England. Her family had money once. No longer. Marisa
is—what do you call it? In French, you say *declassé.*"

"In English, too. What can you tell me about her as
a person?"

"She is beautiful," he repeated. "In Italy, once you
have said that about a woman, there is nothing more to
say."

"All right. Then that's it?" I asked.

"No, there is one other thing." Gaetano's voice
hushed mysteriously. "It may be what you are looking for.
Why you have had me do this?"

He was reminding me that I had left him in the dark.
But I saw no point in enlightening him now. So I simply
said, "It might be. What is it?"

"That car crash—the one in which Peter Winfield
was killed—they say it was no accident."

"You mean it was murder?"

"Or suicide. No one knows. That road near Portofino, it is difficult and winding. But there was no reason for Peter Winfield's car to go over the cliff. He was sober, and he was a careful driver."

"Was he alone?"

"He was *found* alone," Gaetano replied, pointedly stressing the word.

"Were there any witnesses?"

"None. The plot fattens, no?"

"It definitely does," I agreed. "Who would want to kill him?"

"My friends could not tell me that."

"Well, thanks, Gaetano," I said. I decided it was time to bring this expensive transatlantic conversation to an end. "If I need to know anything else, I'll call you."

"I'm at your service, Hank."

"You've done a terrific job. You're a real sleuth."

"Like your Biff Deegan," he said proudly.

"Better," I said. "Much better."

After I hung up, I went over the new bits of information, putting them together with what I already knew. Peter Winfield was a leading authority on Etruscan art. He was murdered. Edgar Greville was about to make a huge killing on the most valuable example of Etruscan statuary to be unearthed in years. Peter Winfield's widow, Marisa, came to see Greville, for some reason, in New York. Greville had her kidnapped.

These pieces of information, these fragments, seemed to want to connect and form some kind of picture. But as yet, I couldn't discern it. I still needed one or two more pieces before I could put it all together and make some sense of it.

Well, my next step was clear enough, anyway. I had to get hold of Carolee Denker.

I looked up the name in the phone book. There was a C. Denker in Chelsea, on West Twentieth Street. That seemed like it might be the girl I was looking for. In New York, attractive women frequently use initials in the phone directory to protect themselves from obscene phone callers.

I was about to try out the listed number. But before I could, my phone rang again. I picked up the receiver. "Hello?"

"Is this Hank Mercer?" a vaguely familiar voice asked.

"Yes. Who's this?"

"This is Greg Blackwell, Hank."

I was surprised, to say the least. After my encounter with Greg Blackwell during the filming of *Kill Me Tender*, I hadn't expected ever to speak with him again.

"Hi, Greg," I said. "How are you?"

"I'm concerned, if you really want to know," he replied. "Concerned about our character."

I didn't take umbrage at that proprietary *our*. At that point, the way I was feeling about it, he was welcome to Biff Deegan.

"But I hear you're already shooting the new film," I said.

"We are," Greg said. "And we're having fights every day. And so I thought—well, you remember, Hank, when we said we were going to get together sometime and have a long talk about Biff Deegan?"

I didn't remember saying it at all. But to be polite, I responded, "Yeah."

"Now's our chance, if you're not too busy. I have some time off, and I happen to be down here in the Village. Only a few blocks from you. I could be at your place in a couple of minutes. Is it all right if I drop by?"

"Yeah, I guess so," I said uncertainly, not hiding my lack of enthusiasm. I had gotten rid of the real Biff Deegan —or as real a one as there was—for the time being. I was in no mood to entertain the sappy movie incarnation of him. "But I have some important business to take care of later on."

"That's all right. I won't stay long. You *are* at this address in the phone book?"

"Yeah."

"Okay," Greg said brightly. "I'll be there with bells on."

I hung up, turned and saw that I was no longer alone. Biff Deegan was standing there, smiling grimly. "I bet he wears bells!" he said.

"I thought you were going to keep out of the way," I said.

"Sorry, I couldn't resist this. Not when you're about to have Greg Blackwell over. I've been wanting to meet that character."

"You know I'm only doing this out of courtesy."

"Sure," Biff said, punching the palm of his hand ominously. "*You* be courteous."

"Look," I said, "if I could have gotten out of it, I would have. I don't want to have to waste time on him. I've got this Carolee Denker lead to follow up. Anyway, after seeing him in *Kill Me Tender*, I don't know what we would have to talk about. I'm not at all happy with him in that movie."

"*You're* not happy." Biff's expression was outraged now. "You're not the one who's being impersonated by a Malibu fruitcake!"

Greg Blackwell had said he would be by in a couple of minutes. As it turned out, it was almost a half hour later when he arrived.

"Sorry, but I was delayed," he said as he came in. "A bunch of fans got hold of me in Sheridan Square. I had to make with the chitchat and give out autographs. It can be a real drag. But what the hell," he added philosophically, "it's all part of the job."

Greg was as pretty as I remembered, and his porcelain smile was as blinding, but he had built himself up alarmingly since I had last seen him in the flesh. When, after doing a brief walkaround in the center of the living room, he came to a stop beside Biff, it was Biff who seemed somewhat puny. It was the sartorial contrast, though, that was striking. Greg, in his blue blazer and polo shirt, was the picture of Beverly Hills elegance. His soft leather brown loafers alone probably cost more than Biff's entire grubby outfit.

Biff edged away from Greg distastefully, and then, doing a little number for my benefit, sniffed at the air around the actor. He wrinkled his nose, as if he were being overpowered by some heavy cologne. Actually Greg was simply wearing a manly aftershave lotion; I had caught a whiff of it when he came in.

"Is this your office, Hank?" Greg asked. "Or do you live here, too?"

Until then, I had thought I had a lavish spread. But seeing it thorough a movie star's eyes, it diminished suddenly to the dimensions of a broom closet. "I live here," I admitted.

"I like this place," Greg said graciously. "It reminds me of an apartment I had near the Strip—when I was starting out."

At that moment, I wasn't feeling particularly hospitable. Still, I asked, "Would you like a drink?"

"No, thanks. I don't drink."

"Some coffee?"

"I don't drink coffee, either."

"Maybe he snorts coke," Biff said.

"I don't take drugs of any kind," Greg said.

"Give this elf some Ovaltine," Biff suggested.

As it happened, I had gone as far as I wanted to with the amenities. I didn't even offer him a chair. To get to the point—and to bring his departure that much closer—I asked, "What's on your mind, Greg? Why did you want to talk to me?"

"Well," Greg said, "we're having an artistic disagreement."

"By *we*, whom do you mean?"

"The director, the producer and me. They want to go ahead with Biff Deegan the way he is in the script now." He was pacing about restlessly, as if he had so much dynamic energy in him he couldn't stand still. "But I'm sorry, it just isn't right." He stopped and looked at me directly. "I thought that maybe if *you* talked to them, you could bring them around to my point of view."

"It depends on your point of view," I said. "What is it?"

"Okay." He paused, as if to gather his thoughts together before he explained. "Now, a lot of people think of Biff as being nothing but a crude slob."

"He better watch his mouth," Biff growled menacingly.

"But as you and I know, Hank," Greg went on, "behind his rough exterior there's an intelligent, sensitive man."

Biff seemed startled now. *This* he hadn't expected.

"He's a decent man," Greg went on, "a basically compassionate man, who believes in justice above all."

Biff looked at me. "Hey, this guy isn't so dumb."

"The real Biff," Greg said, "the Biff I feel I know

better than anyone, would never play a sadistic game of Russian roulette."

Biff's head jerked around. "What?" he asked sharply.

"He wouldn't do what he does in the screenplay now," Greg said. "He wouldn't blow a Mafia guy's brains out just because he won't give him a confession."

"But that's in my book," I pointed out.

"I don't care. A movie is different. That's just too sick a thing for Biff to do."

"Sick!" Biff glared at him. "The creep had it coming to him!"

"I'm sorry, Greg," I said. "But I can't do anything about it. I'm not involved at all in these movies."

"But you can get involved this one time," he said. "They might listen to *you*. You'd have some clout with them. You created Biff Deegan."

"Yeah, but I created a Biff Deegan who plays Russian roulette with hoodlums' skulls."

"You bet your ass you did!" Biff said firmly.

"All right," Greg said, after a moment. He squared his shoulders and furrowed his brow a bit. His tough look; I had seen it in almost every frame of *Kill Me Tender.* "Then I'll have to play hardball with you."

"In what way?"

"You've got points on these movies, right? You're getting a percentage? Well, you're making money on *my* talent."

I just stared at him. "Come again?"

"Do you think the public is buying tickets to see that cliché mug you wrote? They're coming to see *me*. I've built up a following—with my TV series, the other films I've done. Without me, your Biff Deegan would go down the toilet."

"Let me at him!" Biff roared, somewhat illogically.

Even if he hadn't been a hallucination, I wouldn't have held him back.

"I could take a walk on this character," Greg continued. "I could say no to any more sequels. And that would be the end of your gravy train."

Biff went into his jungle fighter's crouch and started to move in on Greg.

"I've spent years building up my image. I'm going to protect it now."

"I'd never dream of tarnishing your image, Greg," I said.

"I realize that, Hank. And there was a time when I might have gone along with the mindless brute kind of thing."

Biff was right beside him now. He went up on his toes and raised his stiffened right hand, ready to bring it down in a fierce karate chop to Greg's neck.

"But that was before I found the Lord."

Biff froze in midchop.

"And thanks to His grace, I'm a more positive and concerned person. I try to live my life according to strict Christian values."

Biff recoiled from him. "Jesus, he's a fucking religious nut!"

"I speak at evangelical meetings around the country," Greg said. "The young people look up to me as an example. I can't disappoint them."

"I don't believe it," Biff said, shaking his head. "I don't believe it."

I sensed Biff's frustration. He was helpless to vent his rage on Greg now. In all my books, I had never allowed him to raise his hand against any religious person. He was scrupulously delicate with all priests, nuns and rabbis—and by extension, it seemed, with all born-again Christians.

"Okay, Greg," I said. "I understand your point and I'll give it some thought."

"Will you speak to them?" he asked.

"Give me a day or two," I said, guiding him toward the door. "Then I'll let you know."

"Fine, Hank," he said, pumping my hand. "We'll be on location all over town. You can come and see me wherever we're shooting."

"I may do that."

I closed the door on Greg and turned back.

Biff still seemed stunned. "I can't take it!" he said. "The whole world thinks I'm *him*." He looked at me despairingly. "Maybe you *should* finish me off."

And suiting his action to the thought, he vanished.

9

The C. Denker in the phone book was, in fact, the girl I was looking for. I found this out through a not very imaginative ploy, one that I would have disdained to use in a book. I called the number and pretended that I was selling subscriptions to *Scientific American*.

The female voice at the other end of the line sounded a little bleary, and then when I stated my business, it turned distinctly cool. The hang-up came when I was no more than two or three sentences into my sales pitch. It didn't matter, though, as I had learned what I needed to know in the very first seconds, when the voice had said that yes, she was Carolee Denker.

And so within a half hour of this aborted conversation, I was standing at her door. Carolee Denker lived in a renovated tenement building that had an unlocked front entrance, and I had been able to climb the stairs to her third-floor-rear apartment without announcing myself. Which was all to the good, since I needed to have the element of surprise on my side. I expected that at her first sight of me, she would recognize me from our encounter at the Hotel Stanhope. I didn't imagine I would be a welcome visitor.

I knocked on the door. I waited, and after a few moments, I heard house slippers shuffling across an uncarpeted floor. The door opened and Carolee Denker looked out at me.

"Holy shit!" she said and tried to slam the door in my face.

I jammed my foot in the door and pushed hard. The door gave way, there was a clatter of slippers as Carolee staggered back, and I was in the apartment.

"It won't do any good to give one of your great performances *this* time, Carolee," I said. "I'm staying. We're going to have a talk."

"What are you?" she asked. "A cop?"

"I might be," I said cagily. "I'm not saying."

She looked me over for a moment. "You're not a cop," she said.

She either was being unflattering or she had sensitive antennae when it came to policemen. I chose to believe it was the latter.

"Okay," I said, "I'm not. But that doesn't change anything with *you*. You're still in bad trouble with the law."

"Yeah?" She tugged absently at a loose strand of hair, gazed blankly at nothing in particular, then shrugged. "It was a gig. I just did my job."

Her indifference seemed genuine enough, and it puzzled me; my first thought was that she might be a little dim-witted. Then I realized that it wasn't her intellect; she simply wasn't in a state to take in the implications of what I was saying—or *any* unpleasant implications, for that matter. Carolee was high on some drug; I was almost sure of it.

The condition of her apartment suggested it, certainly. It was a mess; not dirty, exactly, but awash with the chaotic litter that might be expected in the abode of someone who was too spaced out to put anything in its proper place. Pieces of clothing, household objects, kitchenware, periodicals were strewn over all the available surfaces, including the chair seats and the floor. And Carolee herself, in her discolored house dress and with her unkempt hair, seemed about as slatternly as a pretty girl could be.

"Well, maybe we should discuss it," I said.

"Maybe you should tell me who you are first," she said, eyeing me fuzzily and without real curiosity.

"My name is Hank Mercer."

Suddenly she was alert and attentive. "The guy who wrote *Bloodnight Express?*"

"The book, yes."

"They're casting parts for that movie right now, aren't they?"

"I suppose they are."

"Well, what do you know!"

Carolee smiled broadly, with bright-eyed wonderment and with a touch of practiced flirtatiousness. She may have been stoned, but, evidently, she could get herself together when there was an acting prospect at hand. "Would you like something to drink?" she asked. "Or some coffee?"

"Neither, thank you."

"All right," she cooed amiably. "Then let's make ourselves comfortable."

She sat on the daybed, picked up a pile of magazines from it and patted the cleared area, indicating that I should sit there with her. I did so.

For a moment, I just studied her. She did look a little like Marisa Winfield, but I saw that it wasn't a particularly strong resemblance, now that her hair was no longer in the geometric hairdo and the color of it had reverted to a much lighter shade. The success of her imposture, I realized, had been due more to skill than nature—the hairdresser's skill and Carolee's own skill at makeup.

But she was as attractive as Marisa Winfield, in her own way—a more basic, earthy way. Her body was fuller and more sensual, and at that moment, she was giving me teasing glimpses of it. Her housedress had hiked up to reveal a portion of her bare thighs, and the top of it had somehow opened to provide a view of cleavage.

It was an impressive view, and I wasn't the only one who was struck by it. Biff Deegan was now standing beside Carolee, looking down at her with a lewd smile.

"Nice pair of knockers," Biff said appreciatively.

I was panicked for a moment. But then I caught hold of myself.

I felt determined. I wasn't going to let myself be distracted—not during this crucial confrontation, when I had to have all my wits about me. I put my hand over my eyes and willed Biff to disappear. When I dropped my hand, he was gone.

Carolee was looking at me worriedly. "You all right?"

"Oh, sure," I said. "I was just thinking."

"Look," she said, "if you want me to explain about that number at the Stanhope—what was really going on —I don't think I can help you. I just did what I was paid to do. Nobody told me the reason for it all."

"How did you get hired in the first place?"

"Gary roped me into it."

"Gary?"

"My boyfriend."

"What's his last name?"

Carolee's expression turned wary. "I don't know if I

should tell you," she said. "I mean, you make it sound like something illegal was going on. I'm mad at Gary, but I don't know if I want to get him into trouble."

"Why are you mad at him?"

"He's left town. Just cut out," she said with a little flare-up of indignation, "without telling me."

"Do you know why he's left town?"

"Oh, I'm sure he has a reason," Carolee said darkly. "And it's got a pair of tits and a nice ass."

Her anger was that of a jealous woman, it seemed, not that of a criminal accomplice left in the lurch. "Don't you think it might have something to do with this caper?" I asked.

She looked at me blankly. "What can I tell you? Like I said, I didn't know what was going on. I guess *you* must know something about it, huh?"

"Something. But not enough. I'm trying to find out more."

"Why are you interested?" she asked. "What's all this to you?"

"I know the woman. Marisa Winfield. I'm worried about her." I realized that it was probably useless, but I asked her the Big Question anyway. "Do you know what's happened to her?"

She met my gaze with unaffected innocence. *"Has* anything happened to her?"

"I'm asking *you.*"

"She wasn't a person to me," Carolee said. "Just a role I was playing."

"You weren't told anything about her?"

"Not much. Just that she lived in Rome and that she was a widow. They said I didn't need to know anything more than that, since there wasn't going to be any real dialogue. I mean, I wasn't supposed to talk to anybody or answer the phone."

"Who gave you these instructions? Gary? Or someone else?"

Her expression was guarded again. She drew up her legs, crossed them under her and said casually, "Let's talk about something else." She might have been a hostess directing a conversation to a less boring subject.

"But I want to talk about *this*, Carolee." It was getting harder to conceal my impatience. "That's why I'm here. Now I realize you want to protect your boyfriend—"

"He's not my boyfriend," she cut in.

"I thought you said he was."

"He *was*. Today Gary is just another human being." Carolee gave me her most inviting smile. "Now I don't have any one boyfriend. I'm a free agent. I'm open to all possibilities."

Her housedress seemed to have partly evaporated from her. I was seeing almost completely bare thighs now and half-exposed bosom.

And I saw, to my distress, that Biff was standing beside her again.

"What's with you, dummy?" he asked me. "Don't you know a proposition when you hear one?"

He was right to chide me, of course. I was being slow on the uptake. By this point in a scene, Biff would have had a pliant woman writhing on the bed, begging for a repeat performance.

"You shouldn't have any trouble finding boyfriends," I said to her haltingly. "You're very attractive, Carolee."

"She's a sweet piece of ass, you mean," Biff said. "I wouldn't mind having some of that good stuff myself."

"And you're the sexiest man I've met in a long time, Hank," she purred, leaning toward me.

I remained motionless, not sure what I should do next.

"Go ahead," Biff urged. "What are you waiting for?"

I reached out hesitantly and put my hand on her knee.

"Not on her kneecap, you yo-yo!" Biff said. "Go for her thigh!"

I gripped her bare thigh. It was smooth and very warm. Then I leaned forward all the way and pressed my lips against hers. Carolee responded with startling readiness. She made a passionate little sound and stuck her tongue in my mouth.

That did it to me. For one moment, I was supercharged with lust and capable of anything, any kinky thing I had ever described in my books. Or almost—but then common sense prevailed.

I tore myself away from her, sat back abruptly and looked up at Biff. "No!" I cried out to him. "We shouldn't be doing this! This is serious business!"

"Well, you don't have to yell at me," Carolee said.

I looked back at her. "Oh, I'm not yelling at *you*."

"Who else are you yelling at?" She was visibly upset. "I'm sorry. I thought it was what you wanted."

I glanced around. It was just Carolee and me now. Biff had vanished.

"I guess you must think badly of me," she said unhappily.

"Not at all. I—"

"You probably think I'm trying to put the make on you because I want a part in your movie."

It had almost slipped my mind. In that intoxicated moment, I had let myself believe that she found me irresistible—as Biff was to all the sex-starved women who crossed his path. But now I was brought back to reality. Carolee was, in fact, job-hunting.

"I would *never* think a thing like that," I said. "Anyway, if you want a role in *Bloodnight Express,* there are other ways of going about it."

"How? I can't get any agent to submit me."

"*I* could put in a good word for you," I said.

She brightened. "Could you? Oh, I wish you would! I'm sure there must be parts in that movie that are right for me. I mean, I'm the kind of girl Biff Deegan likes, aren't I?"

"I *know* you are."

"And I'm a good actress."

"You don't have to convince me," I said. "I saw some of your acting at the Stanhope. You're pretty accomplished, I'd say."

"Then you'll do it?" she asked eagerly.

"I might." I paused. "If you tell me what I want to know."

It was put to her squarely. Just a minute before, she had been ready to give me her body for this very same prize. Now I was presenting it as a simpler proposition. All she had to do was betray her boyfriend—or ex-boyfriend, as she would have it. Would ambition or loyalty prevail?

The issue was resolved in about three seconds. "Okay," she said. "What do you want to know?"

"Well, to start with, what's Gary's last name?"

"Halloran," she replied.

"And what does he do for a living?"

"He's a photographer."

I thought for a moment. Gary Halloran. A photographer. I had a feeling I had heard about him somewhere. I couldn't remember in what context, though.

"When did he leave town?" I asked.

"Yesterday. In the evening, I guess."

"And you say he didn't tell you?"

"Not directly, anyway. I talked with him on the phone during the day, and everything seemed normal. We were going to have dinner together. Then, when I got back here around six, I checked my answering machine and there was a message from him. He said he had to leave town suddenly on business and he would be gone for a few days. Business!" she snorted skeptically.

"Maybe he was telling the truth."

"There's only one kind of business that takes Gary away at night." Bitterly she added, "And after I'd gone through that Marisa Winfield routine for him!"

"You did it for the love of him?"

"Well . . . no," Carolee admitted. "For the money. He said it would be worth a thousand dollars to me. It seemed like an easy score," she went on. "I mean, all I had to do was impersonate this Winfield woman for a few days. He gave me a snapshot he had taken of her—"

"One he had *just* taken?"

"Yeah, a day or two before. He'd caught her on a street corner somewhere, when she wasn't expecting it. He said I should imitate her hairstyle and makeup exactly. I was kind of intrigued by the idea," she said with a little smile. "I like to think I'm good at physical characterization. It was a challenge."

"It wasn't Gary's idea, was it?"

"Of course not."

"Then who was he representing?"

"I'm not sure," Carolee said. "I only talked to one other guy. The guy who paid me—and who told me what I was supposed to do at the Stanhope."

"What's his name?"

"I only know his first name. Aldo."

"What does he look like?"

"He's in his forties, fat, going bald. . . ." She shrugged, as if she were at a loss to think of any other meaningful detail.

But she had told me enough. Aldo, I was sure, was the fat man in the blue suit, Marisa Winfield's abductor, the unpleasant fellow who had conked me on the head with the pistol butt.

"Can you tell me anything more about him?" I asked.

"Not much," she said. "Just that he's the building agent where Gary lives."

"Where does Gary live?"

"He has a loft down in Soho."

"And Aldo works for the firm that owns the loft building?"

"Yeah."

"Do you know the name of the firm?"

"Gary mentioned it once or twice. But I don't remember it."

"Would you remember it if you heard it?"

"Maybe."

I tried out the name of the company that owned the Seaview Inn. "Prince Street Enterprises?"

She thought for a moment. "Yeah. That's it. Prince Street Enterprises."

Another piece had clicked into place. Prince Street Enterprises was definitely implicated in the conspiracy. It was, I conjectured, a business front for Edgar Greville's shadowy "financial partners."

"Do you know anything about this firm?" I asked.

"Not a thing," she replied.

"Well, that's all right," I said after a moment. "You've already told me what I needed to know."

"It helps?"

"More than you realize. I'll proceed from here."

"Okay." Carolee eyed me rather morosely now. "Would you do me a favor?" she asked. "If you find out where Gary is, would you tell me? And *who* he's with," she added grimly.

Carolee may have thought her boyfriend was cheating on her, but I had another explanation for Gary Halloran's disappearance.

He had left town suddenly the previous evening. The previous day I had tracked down Marisa Winfield at the Seaview Inn, sending Aldo and Max, with their captive, into flight. Presumably they had gone to still another hideout. The timing of the two things seemed more than coincidental, particularly since Gary Halloran's loft was a Prince Street Enterprises property, just as the Seaview Inn was.

Kidnapping, I knew, was one of the more difficult crimes, in that it required a secure, foolproof hideout in which to confine the victim. The Seaview Inn had been such a place, and another hideout, ideally, would have had to have the same characteristics: an area that had enough space and privacy, in an edifice that was owned or managed by people who were in on the conspiracy— a place, for instance, like Gary Halloran's loft.

Of course, I couldn't be sure how really limited the kidnappers' choices were. Prince Street Enterprises, for all I knew, might have been a far-flung real estate empire. I had to find out about that. And so immediately after leaving Carolee, I went to a pay phone and got the number of the firm from Directory Assistance. I dialed it.

A woman answered, saying the phone number only.

She had a tough Brooklyn voice that was wary from the outset. It was as if she was expecting a complaint.

I pretended to be an apartment hunter in search of a loft. She quickly told me that no lofts were available.

"Are you sure?" I asked. "I was told that Prince Street Enterprises had a lot of buildings."

"You kidding?" she replied. "We only own two loft buildings."

"And that inn out on Long Island?"

"Yeah, and that inn. That's all."

"Oh, I'm sorry," I said. "I guess I was misinformed." I hung up.

My suspicion had become a solid supposition. I thought that there was a good likelihood that Marisa Winfield was now being kept prisoner in Gary Halloran's loft. And that the photographer, who understandably might have felt uncomfortable about it, had elected to remove himself from the situation.

I had arrived at this assumption by sharp, Amos Frisby–type deduction. But it was too soon to feel pleased with myself. My hypothesis still needed some confirmation.

Carolee had told me Gary Halloran's address. I went directly down to Soho to check out his building.

The loft building was on a side street a half block from Spring Street, Soho's main drag. With its funky shops, restaurants and art galleries, Spring was as bustling as ever. But the side street was nearly empty, with few pedestrians and hardly any traffic. It seemed untouched by the renovators. The loft buildings were as unpainted and crumbling-looking as they had been before this neighborhood was discovered by the trend-setters. There was nothing on this street to attract the tourists.

I came to a stop across the street from Gary Halloran's loft building. It was evening now, and here and there up and down the block, lit windows were visible. The lights were on, too, on the fifth floor of the loft building, Halloran's floor.

Someone was there, obviously, but that fact in itself didn't prove anything. One of Halloran's less sinister friends could be using the studio in his absence. I needed a more tangible sign.

I retreated into a doorway, looked up at the empty, lit windows and waited. But I had no luck; ten or twenty minutes went by and there was nothing to see.

Then, suddenly, a familiar fat figure emerged from the front entrance of the building. It was Aldo. He started down the sidewalk briskly, as if he was on some errand.

Even *this* wasn't final proof. Aldo was the building agent, after all. He had legitimate reasons for being there, too.

I glanced up at the fifth floor again, and I had it—the clincher. One of the windows was filled by an enormous silhouette. It was Max, and he was gazing down at Aldo as a housewife would after her departing husband.

I felt sure of it now—where Max and Aldo were, Marisa Winfield was. She was being kept in Gary Halloran's loft.

The problem now was how to get her out.

The name had nagged at me from the moment I had first heard it. Gary Halloran. I knew I had come across that name somewhere before.

I doubted I had read it. He clearly had no great professional reputation; otherwise, he wouldn't have been hiring himself out to criminals. And it wasn't likely that Halloran was of social note, either; Carolee hadn't left me with the impression that her errant lover was the sort who might turn up as one of the Beautiful People in a gossip column.

More probably I had heard his name in some conversation. But, like almost anyone living in New York, I had an overload of names in my brain, and it was taking me awhile to separate this dimly remembered one from the mass of all the others.

And then, as I walked home from Soho, it occurred to me. My friend Windy Grew had mentioned him. I couldn't remember on what occasion. Windy was as much of a Village character as any of the comic types in his caper novels, and his daily talk teemed with the names of the oddball types he encountered in his peregrinations; it was impossible to keep them all straight.

Still, I felt sure that it was Windy who at some time or other had brought up Gary Halloran's name. In which case, there was a chance that he might be helpful.

Finding Windy was no problem. It was Wednesday evening, the evening of the weekly poker game at his place. Until recently, I had been a regular in the game. I knew that the other players, all of them mystery writers like Windy and myself, had been a little sorry when I had dropped out. I had been their favorite pigeon. I could be counted on to lose, but because of my cautious, uncertain style of play, never so much that they needed to feel guilty about it.

My poker-playing colleagues, whenever I ran into them, made a point of telling me they missed me. There was a standing invitation to me to rejoin the game. This was the time, I decided, to do so.

Later that night, I turned up at Windy's door—literally at his door, since Windy had a street level apartment with a private entrance that opened onto the sidewalk. The brownstone he lived in was only a few blocks from mine. While my brownstone was elegant and well kept up, Windy's looked as if it was in some totally different part of town—the territory of a Wyndham Grew novel, perhaps. The building was shabby, gallantly weathered, almost disreputable. Graffiti had been painted on the flaking front wall. There was the name Janie, with a phone number and the promise of delight. Paco and Angel had commemorated themselves in bold white letters.

Windy put on a show of great astonishment when he saw me standing in his doorway. "I don't believe it!" he exclaimed. "I don't believe it!"

He led me into the living room, where the poker game was in progress. "Look at this guy!" he said to the others. "He's like a character in a Russian novel. You can't keep him away from the gaming tables!"

"Make way for Mercer!" Ernie Trasca intoned, drawing in a chair to the space beside him at the table. There was avaricious glee in his eyes.

"Come over here, Hank," Burt Fingerhood said. "The cards are going against me. I want to rub your hump for luck."

"I thought you'd sworn off," Wyatt Shea said to me more seriously.

"I felt like sitting in on a few hands," I said as I took my place between Ernie Trasca and Paul Hubley. "I could be lucky tonight."

"So what else is new?" Paul Hubley asked with ill-concealed envy. He had the worst sales record at the table. "Maybe we can relieve you of some of that Hollywood money."

"It's not good for your character," Ernie Trasca said.

"You guys act like you've never heard of a movie sale before," I commented as I took out my wallet.

"Movie sale?" Burt Fingerhood repeated, arching his eyebrows perplexedly. "I'm still working on the Brazilian comic strip rights on my last one."

I bought a hundred dollars' worth of chips. This seemed more than enough to keep me going in the game until the chance arose for me to talk with Windy alone.

Windy counted out the chips without comment. He hadn't joined in kidding me about my supposed movie wealth. He had had more movie sales than everyone at the table put together, myself included. But no one resented Windy for it, since it didn't show. He continued to live like a Wyndham Grew hero, as if he were an impecunious rascal who survived by his wits. It wasn't an act; he didn't have a hidden fortune in a numbered Swiss bank account. Instead, as we all knew, he had three ex-wives, with a sprinkling of growing children among them.

The game was seven-card stud, and the first few

hands dealt me were, as usual, rotten. I stayed in beyond wisdom a couple of times but could come up with nothing better than a low pair.

At that point, Ernie Trasca was the big winner, and he was enjoying the experience immensely. As he displayed a winning hand, he would snort out an obscenity jubilantly, and then, raking in the pot, he would let out a great, triumphant cloud of smoke from his cheap cigar. The stogie-smoking, along with his propensity for swear words, was a recent affectation with Ernie. He had created a gay detective, and he had adopted these macho characteristics so people wouldn't get the wrong idea about him.

Finally I took in a pot. But I had had a pair of kings showing early and I didn't end up getting much out of it.

My cards turned cold again, and even though it was only a dollar-ante game, it wasn't long before I was fifty dollars down, with Windy still showing no sign of being about to leave the table. But there were only a couple of bottles of beer left. Soon, I hoped, Windy would have to go to the kitchen for more.

Then a poker miracle happened. I was dealt a straight, four through eight, in my first five cards. I tried not to give it away, going along with seeming apathy with the white chip bet on that round. Burt Fingerhood, Wyatt Shea and Paul Hubley were still in.

On the sixth card, Burt Fingerhood, who had a pair of sevens showing, tossed in a two-dollar blue chip. Wyatt stayed in and Paul dropped out. I raised the bet two dollars. Burt went along with it.

Wyatt, after some agonizing, tossed in the extra blue chip, too. He looked at Windy, the dealer on the hand, and said, *"Encore."* Wyatt, whose work remained little known in the states, had been discovered in France, and he had taken to using French expressions.

Windy dealt us each a last down card, first Wyatt, then me, then Burt. Wyatt looked at his card. *"Merde,"* he said, and folded.

Burt tossed in another blue chip and gazed at me with studied indifference.

I tried to read Burt, which wasn't an easy thing to do in any circumstances. Small, with delicate, girlish features, he wore cowboy boots and a leather jacket at almost all times. A passionate lover of the ballet and opera, he was easily the most violent writer of any of us. His heroes indulged in bloodbaths that would have left my Biff green at the gills.

Burt picked up his three down cards, put them together and, cupping them in his hands, held them close to his chest. He gazed at them, blank faced but intent, as if he wanted to make sure he really had what he thought he had.

A little act for my benefit? I wondered. Perhaps. He had two sevens showing and he might have a third. But he couldn't possibly have the fourth, since it was part of my straight.

Biff Deegan appeared behind Burt. He leaned forward and peered over Burt's shoulder, squinting at the cards in his hands. He straightened up and, with a little smile, mouthed the words for me. "Queen—ten—deuce."

So Burt *was* bluffing, after all.

I tossed in a blue chip and then followed it with a second one. "Raise you two," I said.

Burt tossed in two blue chips. "Raise you another two," he said.

I called him. Burt nonchalantly threw the cards onto the table faceup. Three aces. He had a full house, aces and sevens.

I glared at Biff. He gave me his I'm-only-a-hallucination shrug and disappeared.

Windy rose. "I'll get some more beer," he said. He started toward the kitchen.

I excused myself, rose and followed Windy into the kitchen. He had the refrigerator door open when I joined him. Assuming I was there for more beer, he held out a bottle to me.

I took it, then said, "Windy, I'd like to talk with you."

"Sure," he said. He looked at me expectantly.

I paused. The poker game was nearby, and the players' comments as the next hand was dealt were distinct. I knew they could hear us easily, too.

"Privately," I said.

Windy took a bottle of beer for himself and led me into his office, which was at the back of his apartment; the room that opened out into the garden. It was the usual writer's workroom, with a large desk, file cabinets, a daybed and bookshelves. The bookshelves were full, but only with Windy's books; sixty-odd titles, written under several names. He had them in every language, including Finnish, Portuguese and perhaps—it wouldn't have surprised me—Urdu.

It was a fairly austere office, with nothing much in it to suggest Windy's genre other than the small ceramic bust of Edgar Allan Poe—the "Edgar" award he had won a few seasons back for the best mystery novel of the year —that was conspicuously displayed on a shelf.

There was just one sinister touch—the blackjack he used as a paperweight. This blackjack was now resting on a sizeable stack of manuscript. I eyed the manuscript with a certain awe. I knew that Windy had just delivered a new book, and yet this looked close to being still another completed novel. Windy's productivity could be intimidating.

Windy sat on the edge of his desk, unscrewed the cap

from his bottle and took a swig of beer. To be sociable, I did the same.

"What's up?" Windy asked.

I got right to the point. "Do you know Gary Halloran?"

"Gary Halloran? The photographer? Yeah, I know him—sort of," Windy said. "Why are you asking? You need another author photograph?"

"I don't need him as a photographer. I need to know *about* him," I said. "And I remembered hearing you mention his name."

"Did I?" He seemed vague about it. "Maybe I did. But it wasn't because he's any friend of mine. I went to a party at his loft once."

It hadn't turned out to be much of a connection, but it was something. If nothing else, Windy could describe the loft for me.

"How did you happen to go to this party?" I asked.

Windy looked at me quizzically. "Do we need to go into the intimate details of my social life?" he inquired mildly.

"I'd appreciate it, in this case."

With a good-humored shrug, he said, "A girl I was going with brought me there."

This girl was another possible source of information about the loft. So I asked, "Are you still in touch with her?"

"She's in touch with *me.*"

He said it with weariness, and also, perhaps, with a bit of self-satisfaction. Windy, for some reason, was dynamite with the ladies. With his thinning, graying hair and steel-rimmed glasses, he was hardly the conventional idea of a male sex object. But women couldn't leave him alone.

"How does this girl know Halloran?" I asked.

"She's his neighbor," he replied.

I picked up on this eagerly. "She lives in the same building?"

"Yeah. Gail has a loft. She's a painter."

"Where in the building is it? Above or below Halloran?"

He seemed taken aback by my question. "I don't know."

"Well, do you remember on what floor she lives?"

He thought for a moment. "On the seventh floor, I think."

"Halloran is on the fifth floor. That means she's above him."

"It follows," he agreed.

"Is she *directly* above him?"

"Of course. There's only one loft on each floor."

It was perfect; more than I had hoped for. I was overwhelmed by my good luck and all I could do was stare at Windy for a moment. My face, doubtless, showed my emotions, because Windy eyed me curiously and said, "I seem to have scored big with *that* one." He paused, then asked quietly, "What's going on, Hank?"

I didn't answer him immediately. I put down my bottle of beer and paced around the room, concentrating, waiting for the details of my plan to fall into place.

They didn't—not then. But a rough draft of a scheme, at least, was forming in my mind. I returned to Windy and confronted him.

"Windy," I asked, "how would you like to be in on a caper that could be out of one of your own books?"

"If I felt like living them, I wouldn't write them," he said. "But what do you have in mind?"

"A woman is being kept prisoner in Gary Halloran's loft."

His eyes widened. "By Halloran?"

"No, not by Halloran. He's cleared out of town. By the bad guys."

"A damsel in distress?" Windy gave me a pained look. "Hank, that's cornball."

"I can't help it," I said. "Sometimes life is cornball."

This philosophical insight was worth about a second of thought to him. Then he asked, "What's the story?"

I hesitated. Was it possible that Windy, after sixty-odd mysteries, was running a little dry? "I'll tell you this much," I said. "The woman is in serious danger. I'd rather not say any more than that. For professional reasons."

"Are you suggesting I'd *steal* from you?" His tone was mock-injured. But the gleam in his eye was just wicked enough to lead me to believe that my prudence was justified.

"As a friend, I'm asking your help," I said. "As one of my chief competitors, I'm not giving you a *clue* as to what the story is. Fair enough?"

"Okay," he said amiably. "But can you tell me why you need me?"

"I really need your friend, Gail. And her loft, as the jumping-off point."

"For the daring, hair-breadth rescue?"

"That's right."

His shrewd eyes were holding on me as if he were waiting for the joke to manifest itself. "You know," he said, "I don't believe any of this."

"You don't have to. Not yet."

"What's my role in this story? The lovable sidekick?"

"What else?

Windy pondered it for a few moments. But I knew his decision wasn't really in doubt. He was a mystery writer to the core, and I had made him an offer he couldn't refuse.

"I'm not happy about being kept in the dark," he said. "But all right, I'll go along with you on this." The wicked gleam came back into his eyes. "I'll just be observant."

— 11 —

The loft was, as Windy had said, on the seventh floor, two floors above Gary Halloran's loft. It was, along with Halloran's loft, one of the few lofts in the building that were actually lived in; the rest were still being used by small businesses.

Gail, the occupant, was a painter, but she had given the place the homey look of a Victorian house. The plentiful furniture, I assumed, had been in her family for several generations. Except for the unframed canvases on the walls—figurative works of no great distinction—there was nothing about the loft that made it feel particularly bohemian. It was the abode of a middle-class single lady, comfortable, well kept, with everything in it organized.

Gail herself, however, was at that moment coming unstrung. Windy had prevailed on her to cooperate with us. She had been good-natured and helpful so far. But now, as Windy fastened the end of the rope at the base of the radiator, she was having second thoughts.

"Are you really going through with this?" she asked plaintively.

"I'm not doing this for the practice," Windy replied. He was putting together an elaborate knot. I just stood there, watching him. I wasn't very good with my hands in the best of circumstances, and at that point, nervous as I was, I would have been hard put to tie my shoelaces.

"But what will happen to *me?*" Gail asked. She was a trim redhead who was, in all respects, attractive, except for her high, nasal voice. It came across as a whine even when she wasn't upset. "Aldo is the building agent. I pay rent to him."

"Well, he's not there now," I said.

We could be sure, at least, of that much. Throughout the day and that evening, Windy and I had taken turns keeping watch on the building. Max, who seemed to be Marisa Winfield's inseparable jailer, had never left Halloran's loft at all. Aldo had gone in and out. He had just departed again, a half hour before, to perform whatever nocturnal business he had.

"But he'll find out," Gail said.

"You have a lease, don't you?" Windy said. "He can't break it."

"You don't think so? He breaks kneecaps; he can break a lease."

I gave Gail my full attention now. "You know for a fact he breaks kneecaps?" I asked.

"Well"—she paused uncertainly—"everyone knows Aldo's Mafia."

"Which is all the more reason, Gail," Windy said, "that we should rescue this poor girl from his clutches."

"But no one's told me what's going on," Gail protested rather desperately.

"It's drugs. Right, Hank?" Windy asked, giving me a sharp look. He had been fishing all evening.

"Maybe it is and maybe it isn't," I answered noncommittally.

Gail looked at both of us, then stared at Windy in astonishment. "Don't tell me *you* don't know what this is all about, either!"

"My friend Hank assures me that a woman is in danger. What else does a concerned citizen need to know?" Windy asked virtuously.

Gail shook her head unhappily. "I shouldn't have let you talk me into this, Windy."

But there was no real fight in her, I recognized. She would have ultimately done anything Windy had asked. His hold over women was as inexplicable to me as ever, but at least it was working to our advantage.

Windy had finished tying the knot. He rose, uncoiled a few yards of the rope and looped it around a wall pipe for further security. I came over to take a closer look.

"This should hold your weight," Windy said. "By the way, do you know how to shinny down a rope?"

"No," I replied.

"That's all right," he said cheerfully. "I don't know how to tie knots, either."

He stuck the end of the rope through the open window and then played out the length of it until it was taut. I went to the window and poked my head out. The rope was hanging down the side of the building, past the dark windows immediately beneath us, to a point just below the row of windows on the fifth floor.

I checked the street. It was past ten now and it was empty; no traffic, no pedestrians. Most of the windows in the adjoining buildings were dark. This industrial loft block still had only a modest number of live-in residents.

Everything was as it should be. But the sidewalk, as I looked down at it, seemed very far away. I had never really noticed how long a drop seven stories could be.

I stepped back from the window and simply gave
Windy a nod of approval. My throat was suddenly too dry
for me to say anything.

From behind us, Gail asked, "Is there anything *I* can
do?" Last-minute compunctions or not, she was still prepared to be helpful.

"Yeah, Gail," Windy said. "Stand out by the front
door. If you hear someone coming up the stairs, warn us.
It could be Aldo."

Gail hurried off, grateful, I was sure, that she didn't
have to watch me risk my neck.

Windy looked at me questioningly. "Ready?" he
asked. His dubious smile suggested that he didn't think it
likely I was.

And he was right. I was dressed for night climbing in
a black sweater, black work pants and black Keds; my
hope was that this would make me less visible to the
neighbors and to any policemen that might happen by.
And I had Windy's blackjack tucked into my pocket. But
how ready could a flabby, middle-aging novelist be to
carry out a deed of reckless derring-do he had seen only
in movies? Like all Walter Mittys, I was a superman in my
fantasy. But I was confronted with reality now, and the
reality was that I would be staking my life on muscles that
hadn't been used practically in many years.

"I'm not sure," I answered.

"It's up to you," Windy said, with a shrug. "It's *your*
damsel in distress."

When it was put that way, I could no longer hesitate.
I had made Marisa Winfield my responsibility, and this
seemed the only way to save her. It wasn't a time for
self-doubt.

I took a deep breath and clambered onto the windowsill. I gripped the rope in my hands, and abruptly, as

one would plunge into ice-cold water, slid off the window-sill and let myself hang.

I almost lost my grip in that first moment, and would have if Windy hadn't seized me by the upper arms. "Can you make it?" he asked worriedly.

"I can make it," I muttered, though I was no longer so sure. I had the rope between my knees now and I was able to start working my way down in a slow shinnying movement. It took me a few seconds before I could coordinate my hands and knees properly, but then I got the trick of it and started making more rapid progress.

I had enough strength, it turned out; the unexpected problem was the pain in my hands. A life of strictly mental work had left me with palms as delicate as a princess's, and as the rope bit into them, I wanted to scream in agony. I had only been on that rope thirty or forty seconds, but I was beginning to think, desperately, that if I didn't find a footing soon I would have to let go.

At last, my feet made contact with the thin ledge on the fifth-floor level. I let go of the rope and pressed myself against the side of the building, clutching at the bricks.

I was too terrified at first to look in any direction—particularly not down. But I knew from the original lie of the rope that I had come down a couple of feet to the left of a lit, half-open window. Turning my head very slowly so as not to disturb my precarious balance, I looked to my right.

Biff Deegan was on the other side of the lit window. He was standing on the ledge, facing out, lounging nonchalantly. He turned his head toward me and an amused smile came onto his face.

"Look at him!" he said. "The human fly!"

I was so startled that I reacted physically and suddenly found myself wavering unsteadily on the ledge. I recovered my balance and shifted my feet to get a more stable position. As I did so, my right foot slipped off the ledge.

"Watch out for that first step," Biff said. "It's a bitch."

I flung myself forward against the side of the building and dug my fingernails in. I managed to get my right foot back up onto the ledge. Then I stayed absolutely still for a few moments, with my face against the bricks, my eyes closed, and waited for my rapid breathing to subside.

I decided that I would have to ignore Biff, pretend he wasn't there. I opened my eyes and started working my way along the ledge, inch by inch, toward the window. I focused on the bit of window frame that was directly before me. Biff was there, on the periphery of my vision, but I paid no attention to him.

Finally I was right up against the window frame. I leaned to one side and peeked in.

Max was sitting at a table directly opposite the window, reading the *New York Post*. Even doing something this innocent, he seemed hulking and menacing. I had a good view of him at his ugliest angle, in quarter profile, and I could see the hole where his ear used to be.

Only a portion of the loft was visible to me, but I could tell that it was fairly bare, minimally furnished, as a photographer's studio would be. Marisa Winfield, I assumed, was somewhere in there with Max; it was likely that he was keeping her within his sight. If so, she was out of range of my vision.

I withdrew my head and found myself looking into Biff's eyes. He, too, had been peering into the window. The set of his jaw was determined; his gaze was bold and fearless. He was clearly eager to go ahead with the operation—which was more than I could say for myself at that moment.

Still, it was the reason I was there, balancing precariously on that ledge. I had gone that far; I couldn't turn back now.

I slid over my left hand and clutched the brick edge near the window frame to steady myself. Then I shifted my position, turning until I was at an angle to the side of the building.

I knew that Windy was watching me from the window above. I took the blackjack out of my pants pocket and waved it twice in the air. It was my prearranged signal to Windy, letting him know that he should proceed with the next step.

I waited. I imagined Windy lighting the fuse of the giant firecracker, holding it in his hand until it had burned almost all the way down. I hoped he wouldn't panic and botch it.

He didn't. There was a deafening explosion in the air just a few feet below me. Windy had dropped the lit firecracker, timing it so precisely he had almost blown off my toes.

If I hadn't been braced for it, I would have jumped right off that ledge. Instead, with the acrid smell of the firecracker in my nostrils, I kept still and listened— though at first I wasn't sure I had any hearing left. After a moment, I heard a chair being pushed back. Then there was the sound of Max's heavy footsteps as he came toward the window.

I pressed myself back against the brick, trying to keep out of sight. Max leaned out the window and with his hands on the windowsill looked down at the street, searching for the source of the explosion. It was as if his head were being served to me on a platter. It was a little below the level of my waist, and the back of it was totally exposed.

I raised the blackjack and focused on a spot at the base of his skull. Then I froze.

"Go ahead!" Biff said from the other side of the window. "Slug him!"

But I couldn't. I was urging myself to go through with the action. But something in me balked at the brutality of it. I remained motionless, with the blackjack poised in mid-air. I couldn't move any part of my body; I was as fixed as a statute.

I sensed the sudden alertness in Max as he became aware that someone was beside him.

"You're hopeless!" Biff said, taking out his own black-jack from the inside pocket of his sports coat.

Max reared up and twisted around. His hands reached for me, but they didn't quite make it. There was the thud of heavy leather striking cranial bone. Then Max's eyes rolled up into his head and he collapsed onto the windowsill.

Biff, as he put away his blackjack, gazed down at the unconscious Max. Then he gave me an annoyed look, as if he was impatient with me for having disappointed him again. "Get him inside!" he snapped.

My paralysis was gone now. I quickly pocketed my blackjack and crawled over Max into the loft. I had a fleeting impression of Marisa Winfield rising from a chair in a corner to stare at me in amazement. But I didn't pause for a greeting. I grabbed Max from behind and pulled him away from the window. I tottered with him in my arms for a moment. It was too much dead weight for me to support, so I let him pitch over onto the floor, easing the fall as best I could. I didn't want the impact to wake him up.

I turned to Marisa. She was rushing toward me excit-edly. She was still clad in the oversize work shirt and jeans she had been wearing at the Seaview Inn; her captors hadn't even been decent enough to give her a change of clothes.

When she came up to me, she opened her mouth to say something. But there was no time for conversation. I quickly took her hand and said, "Let's get out of here!"

I started out of the loft, drawing her after me. She needed no coaxing. We were both running when we got to the door.

I opened the door and stuck my head out to check the situation outside. Windy was clattering down the stairs to join us, but there was no one else around. I took Marisa's hand again and we stepped out into the hallway.

She recoiled when she saw Windy. He in turn stopped and stared at her with great curiosity.

"It's all right," I told her. "He's my friend."

The elevator, I knew, was ancient and slow, so I started down the stairs, with Windy and Marisa close behind me. We ran down the five flights of stairs. When we came out onto the street, we hardly broke stride but kept running for two blocks until we came to a stop on the corner of Spring Street. There were people around us now, going to and from the bustling restaurants; we were safely back in the mainstream of New York City life.

All three of us were winded and we could do nothing for a moment but gasp as we tried to catch our breath. Then I started laughing. Windy did, too. Even Marisa was smiling now.

"Looks like we did it," I said to Windy.

"Damned right we did!" he said with elation. "That was very exhilarating."

"Are you all right?" I asked Marisa.

"Yes, yes," she said breathlessly. "I'm fine."

Suddenly she was in my arms, hugging me with all

the fervor of her gratitude. I just held her for a few moments, feeling the warmth of her body against mine, the
rapid beating of her heart.

It was a heady moment of intimacy, with exciting
promise to it. When we separated and I glanced at Windy
again, he seemed to have become a little extraneous.

"I guess Marisa and I can go on from here," I said.
"Thanks, Windy."

"Yes, thank you," Marisa said to him, "whoever you
are."

"Wyndham Grew, ma'am," he replied gallantly. "At
your service."

"And I'm Hank Mercer," I said.

"I know," she said. "They told me."

Windy was still standing there. *He* wasn't about to
leave, that was for sure. It wasn't in his nature to walk
away from a beautiful girl. And his unsatisfied writer's
curiosity had to have become a torment to him by then.
It had been an exciting evening, but also, from his point
of view, I knew, a mystifying one.

I remembered I still had some of his property. "Oh,
I almost forgot," I said, and removed his blackjack from
my pocket.

Windy took the blackjack and looked down at it for
a moment. Then with wonderment he said, "Boy, you
really conked that guy!"

I was suddenly confused. "*I* did?"

"A side of you I never figured," Windy said.

I thought back to that moment on the ledge. I realized now that I hadn't actually seen Biff slug Max with his
blackjack. I had assumed it, but. . . .

"Yeah," I said uneasily, and turned and walked away
before we could talk about it further.

I took Marisa by the arm. "Well, see you around," I said to Windy over my shoulder.

"Hank—"

I turned back to him. He had a humble, supplicant's smile on his face.

"You think you could let me in on the story now?" he asked.

"I'll send you a free copy of the book," I said.

I walked on with Marisa into the Soho night.

12

I knew we couldn't go to my apartment. It would be the first place that Aldo and Max—and whatever other hoodlums were working with them—would look for us. At the same time, it was clear that we had to get off the streets quickly. As Marisa and I walked along Spring Street, I was painfully aware of how exposed and vulnerable we were.

I remembered that there was an Italian restaurant nearby, in the south Village, that had a large garden area in the rear. This outdoor dining area, as I recalled, was dark, and the tables were set far apart. Also, there was a fence of modest height—I was thinking of every contingency—that could be scaled in case we had to make an emergency exit.

Within five minutes, we were there. I asked the waiter for a private table in the back. He smiled meaningfully, assuming we were having a romantic tryst, and led us out to a small table in the rear corner of the garden; it was right up against the vine-covered fence. The dining hour was over, so there was no one at the nearby tables. And it was as murky as I could have wished.

We ordered cappuccino. I had already established to my satisfaction that Marisa was suffering no ill effects from her confinement. Her captors hadn't physically mistreated her at all. And now that we were sitting at a restaurant table in a relaxed atmosphere, she seemed as composed as if we were, in fact, on a casual date. She looked completely in place; the jeans and work shirt would have been a standard outfit for a reasonably liberated Village girl. She was wearing no makeup, but with her heavy eyelashes, flawless complexion and full, red lips, she required none.

Our cappuccinos were served. Marisa took an eager first sip of hers; it was as if this beverage was something she had particularly missed in her captivity. Then she looked at me thoughtfully and said, "You went to great lengths to rescue me." Her faint smile was quizzical. "Any reason?"

"You sent me a message at Le Perigord," I replied. "You asked me to help you." With my best nonchalant shrug, I concluded, "I helped."

"Even though I was a total stranger to you?"

"Yes."

"I see." Her voice was a bit lower than I had imagined and rather musical. She could take two small words and hit three distinct notes with them. "Have you learned something about me since then?"

"Not too much," I said. "Just that your name is Marisa Winfield. You live in Rome. You're a widow. And your late husband was an art expert."

She raised her cup to take another sip, but her large, dark eyes held steady on me. When she put her cup down, she looked away uncertainly for a moment, as if she were debating what she should say next.

At length, her gaze met mine again. "I can let you know something more," she said quietly. "My husband was murdered."

This didn't come as too great a surprise to me. Gaetano Bruneschi had suggested as much when he had reported on the Winfields.

I looked at her inquiringly. "That car crash near Portofino? It wasn't an accident?"

"It was no accident."

"Why was he murdered?"

"I don't know," she said. "His associates wanted him out of the way for some reason."

"His associates?" The term puzzled me; I wasn't sure to whom it referred. "You don't mean other art experts?"

She smiled slightly, as if she was fleetingly and grimly amused by the thought. "Hardly."

"Then who are they?"

"They're scum. Criminals." After a moment, she added, "Smugglers."

"Then this *does* have something to do with *The Etruscan Dancer?*"

Marisa's look was sharp and alert now. "You know about it?"

"I've seen it. At Edgar Greville's apartment."

Her expression turned wary. "You're not a friend of Greville's?"

"Far from it. Until a few days ago, I didn't even know him. But I paid him a surprise visit. I sneaked a look at the statue."

"You knew what it was?"

"I got Greville to explain it to me."

"You must be very clever," she said.

"Resourceful, I suppose. Anyway," I asked again,

"was your husband in some way involved with *The Etruscan Dancer?*"

"Yes. He was working with them."

"Working with whom?"

"The men who smuggled *The Etruscan Dancer* out of Italy."

At last, I had it, the missing piece in the picture, and I fitted it into place. Now I could see the various link-ups.

"Why did your husband get mixed up with smugglers?" I asked.

Marisa gave me the cool look the dumb question deserved. "He needed the money." With a touch of bitterness, she said, "We *always* needed money. But we were in worse shape than usual."

"You were in debt?"

"We lived well. We had a nice house on Appia Antica." She shrugged. "We were about to lose it."

"Was he involved in smuggling before this?"

"No, this was the first time. A farmer dug up *The Etruscan Dancer* near Arezzo," she went on. "His first thought, of course, was to keep the government officials from knowing about it—he wanted to make sure he got some money for himself. So he contacted his local gangster. This gangster in turn went to the professional art smugglers. These men are very sophisticated in their work, but they aren't art experts. They still needed to know exactly what the statue was, and what its value was. That's when they brought Peter into it. He knew as much about Etruscan art as anyone in the world."

"So I heard."

"I don't know what went wrong. Maybe Peter had a change of heart, moral qualms. If the poor man had a fault, it was that he could be weak and indecisive. And maybe the others were afraid that he would go to the authorities. Whatever the reason, he ended up dead at the bottom of a cliff."

She said all this in a matter-of-fact way, with no show of emotion. Her coolness about it could have been off-putting; but I imagined that it was the aftermath of an anguish that had been too great, a widow's grief so intense that it had burned itself out, leaving nothing but the flat ashes of feeling.

Still, I knew it couldn't have been easy for her to go over this painful story with me. And I let a moment pass before I asked the next question—the big question that had yet to be answered.

"Why did you come to New York?"

"To ask for Edgar Greville's help," she replied. "I wanted him to help me find the people who killed Peter."

"Wouldn't it have been more logical to go to the Italian police?"

"I did. But they wouldn't reopen the case. Peter's death was ruled an accident. They wanted to leave it at that."

"So why did you turn to Greville?"

"He was Peter's friend, his patron. He was his dealer, too; he gave Peter his only show in New York. He didn't sell many pieces of his sculpture, but he seemed to believe in him. There was no one—or so I thought—who cared more about Peter than Edgar Greville." Ruefully she said, "I was naive."

"So it seems."

"And I remained naive right up to the last moment. It wasn't until I was in that restaurant, pleading with him to help me, that I realized that *he* was part of the ring, too."

"And then it was too late, right?"

She nodded. "I sensed what was going to happen. But I couldn't do anything about it. I mean, you can't make a scene in a restaurant and claim that people are about to hurt you who haven't done anything yet. But I was sure of it. I saw you at the next table. You looked like a kind man—and you seemed to be taking an interest in me," she added with a brief but very feminine smile. "So I scribbled that message to you on that matchbook cover." With a little gesture, she concluded, "I think you have some idea of what happened after that."

"When you got outside, they forced you into a car?"

"Yes. They drove me to a deserted spot, made me take off my clothes and gave me *these* things to wear." She indicated her soiled work clothes with distaste. "Then that other man, Max, turned up. He drove me out to Long Island, to that inn. Aldo came out there later that day."

She had described the sequence of events fairly completely. But I remained hazy about the motivations involved. Certain things still needed explaining.

"I don't understand," I said. "Why did Greville kidnap you?"

"To keep me from telling my story," Marisa said. "He's about to close his big deal with the Metropolitan for *The Etruscan Dancer.* He doesn't want any scandal to come in the way of the sale."

"And what was he going to do with you after he completed the sale?"

"I don't think he'd made up his mind." She smiled slightly and said, "But it didn't look good for me, did it?"

"No, it didn't," I agreed. Then, more brightly, I said, "Well, you're safe now. We'll go to the police and—"

"No, not yet," Marisa broke in.

I was perplexed by the sudden urgency in her voice. "Why not?" I asked.

"I'm not ready to go to the police yet. I'm waiting for more evidence."

"More evidence? I don't understand."

"It's coming from Rome."

"What kind of evidence?"

"Photographic evidence. It indicates that my husband was murdered. And it may show who the killers are."

"You have pictures?"

"Yes. And please don't ask me anything more. I can't tell you about them," she said firmly. "Not now."

I tried to figure out what this photographic evidence might be. All that came to my mind was that there might be photographs, unknowingly taken by a street photographer or some other bystander, of men lurking around Peter Winfield's car, actually working on it, perhaps, sabotaging it so that the brakes would fail or the steering wheel would lock. And these men might be identifiable as people connected with the smuggling conspiracy.

I could only speculate on this, since she chose to be secretive about it. She had, however, without realizing it, answered another even more intriguing question for me.

"You're waiting for evidence from Rome," I said. "Is it being brought by that person you were expecting at the Stanhope?"

Marisa seemed startled now. "You know I was expecting someone?"

"I deduced it."

"But how?"

"It wasn't difficult," I said without explaining further.

She gazed at me intensely. "You *are* a clever man, aren't you?"

I had impressed her, obviously, and I couldn't help

but be pleased by the new respect I saw in her eyes. But I tried to be modest about it. "I've trained my intellect that way," I said. "It's my business."

She looked at me for another fascinated moment. Then, finally, she answered my question. "Yes, he's bringing the evidence."

"Who is he? Can you tell me?"

"His name is Desmond Corley. He was a friend of my husband."

"Is he in the art world, too?"

"Not exactly. He's a writer, though I don't think he's ever published anything." With a smile, she explained, "Desmond is one of those classic expatriate Englishmen. He gets by on charm and a small check from his solicitor every quarter."

"And he's been helping you?"

"Yes. He has been working along with me to find out the truth. He's as determined to see justice done as I am. Desmond has been wonderful," she concluded with appreciative fervor.

"When is he arriving?"

"Tomorrow morning. So, you see," she said, "it only means waiting another day."

Short as it was, the wait seemed unnecessary to me. Marisa would certainly have been safer in the care of the authorities. And—in one part of me, anyway—I was eager to turn this matter over to the police. Once I had done that, I would have officially won my bet with Norman.

But she seemed determined to do it *her* way; and in the other part of me, I was ready to cooperate with her. It meant that I would have her to myself a little while longer. And I had decided by now that she was the most beautiful and fascinating woman I had ever met.

"All right, we'll wait until tomorrow." Then, gazing at her steadily, I said, "But you're going to have to be more honest with me."

"I *have* been honest with you," she insisted.

"Not completely. You weren't going to tell me about Desmond Corley, were you? About that evidence that's on its way?"

She looked uneasy, then gave me a sheepish little shrug as her answer.

"That happens to be the key to this whole thing," I went on. "Now I understand what's going on."

"What do you understand?" she asked carefully.

"You told Greville about that evidence, didn't you? Even before you had lunch with him?"

"Yes," she said, after a moment.

"Then that's why you were kidnapped. It wasn't just to keep you from telling your story. Greville could have accomplished that simply by having you killed. With two million dollars at stake, it would have been worth it to him. But then there would still have been your friend, Desmond Corley, and the evidence he has. They'd have to kill him, too, and destroy the evidence he has."

Marisa's face was expressionless now. She neither said anything nor did she seem surprised at all. It was as if she had been told this—or had figured it out—already.

"Did you know about the other woman?" I asked. "The one they put in your place at the Stanhope?"

Her eyes widened. Now she *was* astonished. "No," she said softly. "Why did they do that?"

"So that when Desmond Corley arrived, there would still be a Marisa Winfield residing at the hotel."

"Did she look like me?"

"Sort of. And she wore your clothes and did her hair the same way."

"But she couldn't pretend to be me," she said incredulously. "Not with Desmond."

"She wouldn't have had to. She just wouldn't have answered the phone. The switchboard would have referred Desmond to the other number, the Seaview Inn number. He would have called there, and you would have been put on the phone—with a gun in your back. You would have asked him to come out to the Seaview Inn. And the trap would have been set."

Marisa was thoughtful for a few seconds. She seemed to be going over the whole thing again in her head. Then she said, "But that won't happen now. Thanks to you."

"Thanks to me," I said, repeating it pointedly. "So why didn't you level with me in the first place?"

"I suppose I didn't trust you completely yet."

"Will you trust me from now on?"

Marisa smiled, leaned forward over the table and took my hand. "I'll trust you, Hank."

13

I now had to think of a place where Marisa could stay the night—where we both could stay, since I didn't dare go back to my apartment. There were hotels, of course. But we might have had a problem at the better hotels; without luggage and dressed as we were—she in her work clothes and I in my burglar's outfit—we weren't any reservation clerk's idea of a respectable couple. There were no lack of fleabag hotels that would take anybody, but I didn't want to spend my first night alone with Marisa in some seedy dump.

I mentally went through a list of several friends I could call who had spacious apartments, and then I ruled them all out. At that point, I didn't want to involve anyone else in this situation.

It seemed a real dilemma. But then I remembered that my publisher maintained a company apartment in the midtown area. I had been there a couple of times for parties. It was sometimes used to lodge visiting VIPs or to accommodate the firm's own commuter executives when they had to stay in town overnight. I had the impression, though, that it was usually empty.

Norman Wagstaff had access to it, I knew; I remembered an occasion in the recent past when he had put up one of his out-of-town authors at the apartment. It seemed worth giving him a try.

I didn't like the idea of leaving Marisa alone at the table. But it would only be for a couple of minutes, so I told her what I was about to do and excused myself. I went into the interior of the restaurant, sought out the phone and dialed Norman's home number.

It was a quarter past eleven, which wasn't a civilized time to phone anybody, not even a bachelor book editor who wasn't known as an early bird. Norman, though, when he answered, sounded wakeful enough; just grumpy and abstracted, as if the phone had interrupted him in the midst of some absorbing activity.

I quickly explained my reason for calling: that I had just rescued a woman from a Soho loft, that murderous criminals were in pursuit of us, that we needed to hide out that night in the company apartment.

I said all of this in a sustained burst. When I was through, Norman asked, "Hank, are you sober?"

"Of course I'm sober. Norman, I'm not making this up. You remember that bet we made at the restaurant?"

There was a brief silence at the other end of the line. "You mean you've actually found a real-life crime story? Starting with that matchbook cover?"

"I sure have."

"So what are you doing now? Researching it?"

"Researching it? Hell, I'm living it! And it's going to make a dynamite book. A *big* book."

"A big book?" Norman echoed with the reverence that commercial publishers have for those magical words.

He immediately arranged to meet us in a half hour at the address of the company apartment, which was, as I'd expected, unoccupied.

I timed it almost exactly. Thirty-two minutes after I hung up, Marisa and I got out of a taxicab in front of an elegant apartment building on East Fifty-second Street. It was an older, smaller apartment building, a well-constructed ten floors.

Norman was already there, standing by the entrance, waiting. He hurried over to us and I introduced him to Marisa.

It was as if Norman were setting eyes on her for the first time; evidently he had barely noticed her at Le Perigord. He was appropriately suave with her. But his gaze was bright with curiosity. I doubted that he was disappointed in what he was seeing. Marisa's dark, dramatic beauty promised much: mysteries, unexpected revelations, emotional climaxes. Norman had to respond to it; he could have been looking at the face on the cover of one of his own romantic suspense novels.

He led us into the building and took us up to the eighth floor in a self-service elevator. He unlocked the door of the company apartment, then stepped back to let us go in first.

It was a fairly standard modern apartment, with an L-shape living room–dining area, one large bedroom and a terrace. I was ready to accept it as it was, but Marisa wanted to inspect it, so I followed her about as she did so. She suddenly seemed a hard-to-please apartment hunter. The place had a homogenized luxury to it; the interior decorator had taken no chances anywhere—everything was safely Bloomingdale's or W&J Sloane. You would have thought that, considering her accommodations of only a few hours earlier, Marisa would have been grateful for the functional, if bland, comfort. But what I got from her expression now was a discreetly veiled distaste; it was clear that she would have done the apartment very differently.

When she was through with her tour, she turned to Norman and me and announced crisply, "The first thing I'm going to do is take a bath." And she headed toward the bathroom.

I accompanied Norman out into the hallway. He gave me the key to the apartment.

"Thanks, Norman," I said. "I really appreciate this." We walked together toward the elevator. "Did I take you away from a manuscript?" I asked.

"From an old Bette Davis movie—which is worse."

"Well, I hope I didn't put you out too much."

"It's quite all right." He stopped by the elevator and just looked at me for a moment, benign and perplexed at the same time. "When are you going to tell me what this is all about?"

"Soon," I said. "Be patient."

"You say it's a big book?"

"A blockbuster. A front-page news story." Brightly I added, "What more could we ask for our first Amos Frisby book?"

It was a reminder to him that I had won our bet, and Norman gave me a tight smile in acknowledgment of it. "How's Frisby doing?" he asked.

"He's been dazzling. One brilliant deduction after another."

"And no violence?"

"Well"—I hesitated as I remembered, with some uneasiness, the thud of that blackjack on Max's skull—"it's a violent world."

"You got a title?"

"The Etruscan Dancer."

He stared at me. "The *what?*"

"It will all be explained," I said quickly. "Now I have to get back to Marisa. Good night."

I turned and went back to the apartment, bearing

with me the image of Norman's expression as he stood at
the elevator—baffled, pained and intrigued.

Marisa adjusted the bathrobe, closing it over her
chest to keep out the slight chill that was in the night air,
and went on with the story of her life.

We were sitting out on the terrace, with the drinks
I had fixed for us at the well-stocked bar; a vodka and tonic
for Marisa, a Scotch and soda for me. We had both bathed,
but there had been only the one man's bathrobe hanging
in the bathroom. Marisa was wearing it and I was dressed
in my street clothes again.

She took a sip of her drink, then gazed before her as
a moment of punctuation before she came to the climax
of her story.

"My father was found guilty," she said. "He was sen-
tenced to ten years in prison."

"Is he still there?" I asked.

"He will be up for parole in a few months. I imagine
they'll let him go. Daddy has always been very persua-
sive."

I had gathered as much from her story.

Marisa's father, or so she had told me, had once been
a highly respected international financier, an establish-
ment type who had gone to all the right schools and who
had all the right New England antecedents. For whatever
reason—it might have had something to do with Marisa's
mother, an Italian woman who, as her daughter charac-
terized her, had both great beauty and extravagant tastes
—he had carried out a gigantic swindle. From what little
she had told me, I guessed it was some kind of pyramid
scheme in which the manipulator, by paying out substantial profits to his initial investors, lures a large number of

victims into buying worthless securities. The structure he had created had ultimately collapsed. The scandal had been resounding, the disgrace intense; and the family had been totally ruined.

Marisa had fallen silent and she was looking out moodily at the view—what there was of it. There was a rectangle of open space between two taller buildings, and we could see a short distance, as far as the massive modern apartment building on the next block.

At length, she said, "It's best never to have had any money."

"Most people wouldn't agree," I commented.

She looked at me challengingly. "You think it's better to have been raised the way *I* was—in beautiful surroundings, spoiled by my parents, given everything I wanted—and then have it all taken away?"

It didn't seem one of the more compelling social problems. But I knew I couldn't make her understand that. "So, all right," I said, "you adjust. And maybe it was all for the good. It meant you had to create a life of your own."

"I tried to," she said with a wan smile. "By doing absolutely the wrong thing."

"Which was?"

"Getting married, too young."

"You didn't love Peter?"

"In the beginning, I suppose," she replied. "And now I love him a little again, in retrospect. But in between, there were all those poisoned years."

"What poisoned them?"

"His unhappiness."

"Why was he unhappy?"

"He thought he was a failure."

"But he was a recognized art scholar, wasn't he?"

"He was a *great* scholar," she said. "He could have had a job with any museum in the world."

"He was that important?"

"Yes. You see, he was more than just an art expert. He was a brilliant scientist."

"Oh? What field was he in?"

"He was trained as a chemist. But he used his science in his art research. In his studies of Etruscan art."

"In what way?"

Marisa seemed a little reluctant to answer now. I had the feeling that for some reason she was sorry she had told me even this much. "Do you really want to hear? Most people don't find it that interesting."

"I find it *very* interesting," I said. "Please, tell me."

After hesitating for another moment, she went on. "Peter developed the tests and found the chemical formulae that the leading museums now use to authenticate Etruscan art. He determined the exact chemical composition of Etruscan bronze. More than that, he went to all the Etruscan sites in Italy and did a thorough analysis of the soil at each place, testing for the amounts of the different substances in it—lead, arsenic, iron, the various organic plant materials. And so, finally, he was able to pinpoint any Etruscan piece in both time and place."

"Through the soil?"

"Yes. The soil is absorbed in the patina of a metal statue. It leaves a chemical imprint that can be read—or could be read by Peter, anyway. Take *The Etruscan Dancer*, for instance," she continued. "A few of us know when it was dug up and where. But let's say it had appeared on the market out of nowhere, with no known history. Peter, with his tests, would have been able to establish not only its age but also that it had been lying in the ground near Arezzo."

"That's remarkable," I said.

"Yes, I know. Everyone thought it was remarkable," she said. "But it meant nothing to Peter. He considered it dry academic work. He saw himself as an artist. It was all he really wanted to be. And as a sculptor—I have to say it"—she shrugged unhappily—"he was mediocre."

"Who said so?" I asked, instinctively bridling. I was automatically on the side of all maligned creators. "Critics?"

"Anyone who knew anything about sculpture said it. Peter executed every piece beautifully. But that certain ingredient was never there." Marisa was thoughtful for a moment. "What a difference that one thing makes!" she said. "Talent." She gazed at me. "You're lucky."

"Me?"

"You were born with a gift. You're a successful artist."

"Oh, I—" I stammered as much from surprise as modesty. I had been waiting for fifteen years to hear that word applied to me, and now it caught me unprepared. "I wouldn't call myself an artist."

"But you are," Marisa said. "I've heard of you. I've seen your books in Italy."

I remembered Gaetano Bruneschi's eccentric way with language and quickly said, "Yeah, but I think I'd rather have you read them in the original English."

"All right," she said. "Which one should I read first?"

"The one I'm about to write."

She seemed a little taken aback. "None of the others?"

"I'm not sure you'd like them," I said. "They all feature this private-eye hero. He's kind of a crude type; you might not relate to him. My new hero, in my new book, will be more your kind of man."

"What will he be like?"

"Cultivated. Stylish. Brilliant."

Marisa smiled. "Like you?"

"Well . . . maybe."

She leaned toward me. "And will he be strong? Like you?"

Her bathrobe had opened at the bosom again, and the scent of the soap she had just used was filling my nostrils. It was dizzying. "Am I strong?"

"You're heroic," she said softly, gazing into my eyes. "It was wonderful, the way you came after me and saved me. I've never met a man like you."

Our heads were close together now. A few inches closer and our lips would have been touching. But I held still, neither moving toward her nor away.

I had professional hesitations. I didn't know if I should get sexually involved with her. She was, after all, the heroine of the book I was about to write; it might endanger my artistic objectivity.

But she wasn't seeing me as a remote, impersonal novelist, I realized. I was Amos Frisby to her. And Amos Frisby wasn't a stone. For all his intellectual gifts, he was a virile, animal male, a man who needed a woman. Marisa was the stylish beauty he deserved; if she was the prize he had won, he would take her.

I kissed her. She put her arms around me and made it last. It was tender and at the same time sharp with the hunger of a kiss long overdue.

From there, it was a short, direct path to the bedroom, and five minutes later, we were on the bed, with the blankets discarded. Marisa was lying on her back, naked, her eyes closed, her lips parted, and I, stripped to my shorts, was kneeling over her, worshipping her. I wasn't ready yet to join with her. The perfection of her body was too intimidating.

Instead, I approached her by degrees, absorbed the physical wonder of her bit by bit. I kissed her neck, then her shoulders, then her lovely, firm breasts.

"Beautiful!" I heard a deep, rough voice say. "Beautiful!"

Horrified, I flipped onto my side and looked up. Biff was standing right over us. His blood-rimmed eyes as he stared at Marisa were smoky with lust; I had never seen his expression so depraved.

"Don't let me stop you," Biff said. "I'll just watch."

I quickly drew the sheet up to Marisa's neck, covering her.

"What's the matter?" she asked.

I looked at her, momentarily at a loss for an answer. "Oh—it's a little cold," I said.

Marisa was puzzled. "Cold? *I* don't think so."

I glanced up again. Biff was gone.

But I knew he would reappear. And knowing that, I couldn't go forward. I couldn't even enjoy Marisa's company in the most innocent way—not with that leering presence hovering over us.

And Biff, I was sure, was doing it deliberately. I couldn't let this go on any longer, I decided. I had to have it out with him, once and for all.

"Excuse me for a minute," I said to Marisa and rose from the bed. Her expression was bewildered, but I didn't pause to explain; nor did I stop to put on any clothing. In my shorts and barefoot, I padded out to the living room.

Biff was waiting for me. He was lounging against the back of the couch with the irritating, wise-guy smile on his face.

I confronted him angrily. "Listen," I said, "I've put up with a lot from you, but I'm not putting up with *this*. Not with her."

"What's the big deal about her?" he asked. "She's just another broad."

"She's not a broad. She's a woman. She's *the* woman."

He sucked on his molars skeptically. "Yeah?"

"Yeah. The woman I've been waiting for all my life. I sensed it when I saw her at the restaurant. And now I know it."

Biff looked annoyed. "What *is* this bullshit? Ball her, if you want—but don't play a fucking violin for me."

"You can't understand, can you?" His sneering tone infuriated me, and it was all I could do to keep from yelling at him. "A woman is just a slab of meat to you. Well, this thing I have with Marisa is beautiful and sacred. And I'm not going to let you defile it!"

"Defile?" He threw up his hands to protest his innocence. "I was just taking an interest."

"*That* kind of interest I can do without." I paused and then said it, evenly and with firmness. "This is it, Biff. We're parting ways here and now."

He just looked at me for a moment. "You really mean it, don't you?"

"Yes, I do," I said. "I guess, in some crazy way, I must have needed you. But I don't need you anymore."

"Now that you have this broad?"

"Yeah. Now that I have this broad."

His expression was serious now, almost contemplative. I knew that he understood it as well as I—that there wasn't room for both Marisa and him in my life.

"You're making a mistake with that girl," Biff said quietly.

"I don't think so. Anyway, it's my choice, not yours. So just go, Biff." With soft intensity, I repeated it. "Go!"

He shrugged resignedly, accepting his fate. In this last moment, I had to admire his stoic courage. He was being a man about it. Biff was tough to the end.

"Take care of yourself," he said.

Biff started to fade slowly. His texture softened, the colors of him started to blur together and then he became transparent. His face grew indistinct, shadowy.

I felt a sudden pang of regret. I had an impulse to reach out my hand, to catch hold of him while some part of him was still there. But I stopped myself.

Biff spoke again. His voice was hollow now and sounded as if it came from a distance. "It's not too late to change your mind," he said.

"It *is* too late," I said. "Good-bye, Biff."

He vanished. A last wavering silhouette, and then there was nothing.

I stood there for some time, staring at the place in the air where Biff had been. It had been harder than I had realized it would be, more painful.

Then I turned and went back into the bedroom. Marisa was sitting on the edge of the bed, waiting for me. I sat beside her.

"Were you talking to yourself out there?" she asked.

"Yeah." I took her hand. "But I won't do it again. Ever again."

It was our first breakfast together, and it had the blissful, charmed feel of a honeymoon breakfast.

We sat across from each other at the dining table and spooned up warm oatmeal. There had been no perishables in the refrigerator, but we had found the oatmeal, a box of sugar and an unopened can of coffee in the cupboard. Marisa had prepared the cereal to perfection; it had none of the lumpiness of a Betty Ann batch.

Her talent with oatmeal was only one of several differences between her and my ex-wife. A more significant one was the way she looked at that moment. Betty Ann, in her bathrobe, just after rising, had borne an unnerving resemblance to her mother; in the early mornings, she had previewed her drained middle age. Marisa, on the contrary, sitting in her bathrobe at the table, still had her evening face on; fresh, glowing, ready to outdazzle the world. She had woken up with it intact.

She was playful with me while we ate. She took my hand in her free hand and, when her mouth wasn't otherwise occupied, nipped kittenlike at my knuckles, a reminder of the love bites of the night before. I didn't resist at all. In the mood I was in, I would have let her devour me whole. I was happy. It had been a long time since I had been anything but alone at that time of the morning. It seemed lucky beyond belief that my solitude should have been ended by so glorious a creature as Marisa.

I wanted to tell her of my feelings. I wanted to go even further and discuss our future. There was no reason this should be a brief, happenstance affair; we could have a deeper, more permanent relationship. It was premature, perhaps, to be thinking this—though not necessarily. Every time our gazes met, it seemed to me that she was thinking those same thoughts.

She had *something* on her mind, certainly, something she seemed about to verbalize. After she cleared the bowls from the table and poured our cups of coffee, she sat again and with a dreamy smile said, "You know what I want now?"

"What?" I leaned forward eagerly.

"Some clothes," she said. "I wish I had some nice clothes I could put on right now. So I could feel like a woman again."

This mundane note was a bit deflating. I sat back and commented, "You seemed like a woman last night."

"A figure of speech, darling," Marisa said with a smile. "And you know what I mean. I can't be a complete woman without clothes. I wish I could go out to a store and buy a dress. But I can't," she went on with a sad shrug. "Those men took everything. My money, too."

"I have money," I said, taking out my wallet.

When I had embarked on the previous night's adventure, I hadn't known what to expect or where I would end up. So I had brought along a surplus of cash. I counted out some bills now. "Would two hundred be enough?"

"Oh, yes, of course," she said, with a look of happy surprise. "Thank you, darling." She took the money from me and checked through it quickly. "I won't spend it all."

"Spend what you have to," I said.

I rather enjoyed playing the benevolent sugar daddy to her. I could imagine myself buying a whole new wardrobe for her, garment by garment, taking as my reward only her joy and her grateful embraces.

But then it occurred to me that she had a more immediate reason than general vanity for needing something to wear.

"I suppose you want to look your best for your friend," I said. "Desmond Corley. He's coming in today, isn't he?"

"This morning," she replied.

"But you're not at the Stanhope. Where will he go?"

"Desmond and I had that worked out. We knew that something might go wrong. So we agreed that if I wasn't at the Stanhope, he was to go to Grand Central Station. He was to put the envelope—the one that has the evidence in it—in a locker." She recited all this slowly, as if she wanted to make sure she was remembering the details of the plan correctly. "And then he was to stand under the big clock from eleven to eleven twenty. Just on the chance."

"The chance of what?"

"That I could get to him."

"And that's where you'll meet him?" I asked.

Marisa seemed suddenly uncertain. An expression of fear came onto her face.

"I can't do it," she said finally. "I can't go there. After what's happened, I'm too afraid."

The solution was self-evident. "*I* can meet him, if you want."

The fear vanished from her face in an instant. "You *are* wonderful," she said with a warm smile.

I basked in the glow of her admiration for a moment. And then I began thinking about the details.

"If you still want to go shopping," I said, "we have a problem." I glanced at my watch. "It's a quarter past nine. I should be at Grand Central at eleven. And we only have one key."

"That's all right," she said. "I'll take the key. The stores don't open until ten, but I'll still try to be back by the time you leave. If I'm not," she added, "I'll definitely be here by eleven thirty."

"You're sure of that?"

"You think I wouldn't be here to welcome Desmond?" With a welling up of emotion, she said, "Desmond and you are the only people in the world I care about now. The two strong men who have helped me."

I stood under the clock, waiting. It was five minutes past eleven and I had been there five minutes exactly. Desmond Corley had yet to appear.

I was at the end of the main passageway that led into the huge interior of Grand Central Station, and the clock was directly above me. Electronic headlines ran along the base of the clock like ticker tape—the clock was a promotional device for *Newsweek* magazine—but I paid no attention to them. I concentrated on looking, alternately, in the two directions from which Corley might come.

For a few moments, I would look into the interior of the station, at the round information booth in the center, at the escalators that connected Grand Central with the Pan Am building, at the various passageways on both sides. Then I would turn and gaze up the passageway that led to the street. I was in the main flow of traffic and any number of people came toward me. But none conformed to the description of Desmond Corley that Marisa had given me.

I stayed in the appointed spot; though, of course, it made no difference whether I did or not, since Corley wouldn't be looking for me or for anyone but Marisa. I was aware that might create a problem—he would have every reason to be suspicious of me—and I had come prepared for it. After breakfast, just before she had gone out shopping, Marisa had dashed off a note that I was to give to Corley. It assured him that I was to be trusted. I had that folded sheet of note paper in my pants pocket.

The minutes went by—it was nine minutes past the hour now—and I was beginning to wonder if Corley would turn up at all. Had something gone wrong? Could Edgar Greville and his accomplices somehow have gotten to him before he could reach this rendezvous point?

Then I saw him coming down the passageway from the street, a tall, gangly man wearing a tan corduroy jacket and a polo shirt. He matched Marisa's description in every respect. He was handsome and had a full, blond mustache; he was in his late thirties and looked very British. And if I had any doubt about his identity, he himself dispelled it. He slowed down when he saw me staring at him and then came to a complete stop a few yards away and eyed me apprehensively.

I went over to him. "Are you Desmond Corley?" I asked.

"Who are you?" he asked warily.

"I'm Hank Mercer. I'm a friend of Marisa."

I gave him her note. Desmond Corley scanned it quickly. Then he relaxed and thrust out his hand. "It's a pleasure meeting you," he said, giving my hand a hearty shake. "Where *is* Marisa, by the way?"

"She's waiting for us at an apartment," I replied. Actually I wasn't sure of this, since she hadn't returned by the time I had left. So I corrected myself. "She'll be there, anyway, when we get there."

"Why isn't she at the Stanhope?"

"There were complications. We'll explain later."

Corley was gazing at me steadily, as if he were still trying to size me up. "All right," he said. "Let's go."

He took a step as if he was ready to depart, but I stood where I was. "Didn't you bring something with you?" I asked. "Something you've put in a locker?"

He gave me a quick, sharp look. Then he laughed suddenly. "She's told you everything, has she?"

He had a loose-lipped smile, the too-easy smile of a man who thinks he's a charmer. I didn't know Desmond Corley at all. But I had the feeling that even if I got to know him very well, I wouldn't like him a whole lot.

"Yes, she's told me," I said.

"It's in a locker downstairs," Corley said. "We might as well get it."

We crossed the station, heading toward the stairs that led to the lower level.

"Sorry if I seemed unfriendly," Corley said as we walked. "But I've been a little jumpy."

"Have you had problems?" I asked.

"I don't know," he said. "In Rome, at the airport, I had a funny feeling I was being watched."

"Did you see who was watching you?"

"No. As I said, it was just a feeling."

"What about here?"

"Here? I'm not sure. A car stayed behind my taxi all the way in from the airport. But I don't know if it was following me."

We came to a stop at the head of the stairs. Corley turned to me and with his easy smile said, "I should warn you that I'm famous for my paranoia."

We went down the stairs to an underground corridor. It was very long, with a marked incline at one end. The Oyster Bar restaurant was at the foot of the stairs, and a little farther on, at the base of the incline, there was a shoeshine stand. A bank of lockers was against the opposite wall, midway between the two.

The rush hour was long past and there was hardly anybody to be seen up and down the corridor. The restaurant seemed empty. The shoeshine man had no customers.

Corley took out a key, went to a locker and opened it. He withdrew an ordinary, unmarked nine-by-twelve manila envelope. It wasn't thick and bulging. If it contained photographs, there couldn't have been more than four or five of them; and, perhaps, a few sheets of paper.

"This is the evidence?" I asked. "Pictures and all?"

"This is it," he said.

I looked up from the envelope and met Corley's eyes. Then I happened to glance beyond him. What I saw chilled me.

Aldo and Max were coming down the incline, walking toward us rapidly. They were looking at us intently as they approached.

I reacted instantly. "Run!" I cried out to Corley.

I took a first step down the corridor and then, looking back over my shoulder, saw that Corley wasn't following me. He was staring at me with incomprehension. He turned to see what it was that had alarmed me.

That was his fatal mistake. It gave Aldo the time to draw his automatic, plant his feet and set himself in an aiming position, with his left hand gripping his right wrist. It wasn't a difficult shot, and Aldo fired only once.

I heard Corley's strangled grunt of pain and saw him stiffen with the impact. His arms went up as he staggered in the moment before toppling over. I reacted automatically, without thinking of the fact that I was exposing myself to another shot, and snatched the manila envelope as it slipped from his fingers. Then I turned and started running down the corridor.

I ran with all the terror of someone who expects a piece of metal to cut through him at any second. When that didn't happen immediately, I glanced back quickly. Aldo and Max were running after me. Beyond them, I saw Desmond Corley lying in a still heap on the pavement. Farther up the corridor, the shoeshine man was flat on his face.

I tried to increase my speed. I was heading for the stairway to the Lexington Avenue subway, but it was still the length of a city block away. Behind me, I could hear the clatter of shoes on stone; the sound seemed to be holding at the same distance. I wasn't gaining any lead on my pursuers at all.

There was a sharp pain in my chest as I gasped for air, but finally I reached the stairway. Then I made the same mistake Corley had made. I stopped to look back.

Aldo, who was a few steps in the lead of Max—he was fast for a fat man—came to a halt and quickly went into a sideways aiming position.

He fired, but I was gone from the spot a split second before he squeezed the trigger. The double ping of the bullet as it struck a wall and ricocheted served to give me an instant second wind as I raced down the stairs.

I came down onto the subway-station level. There

was the usual line at the token booth, and a fair number of people were passing through the turnstiles in both directions. I didn't have a subway token, and even if I had had one, I couldn't have spared the time to rummage in my pocket for it. Without breaking stride, I vaulted the turnstiles.

"Hey, you!" the token clerk yelled after me.

I stopped and turned back, hopefully. I wouldn't have minded being arrested at that point. But there was no transit policeman in sight. And now I heard the clatter of shoes again. Aldo and Max were coming down the stairway.

I dashed down the steps that led to the downtown platform of the Lexington Avenue subway. A crowd had gathered on the platform, but no train seemed to be coming. I stood there uncertainly for a moment. I only had a few seconds to decide what to do next. And my avenues of escape were reduced to just one.

It was scary, but I had no choice. I jumped down onto the subway tracks.

A woman screamed. A man cried out, "Someone get him!" There was concern in his voice. Perhaps he thought I was a would-be suicide.

I located the third rail—it was safely on the other side of the tracks—then ran toward the uptown entrance of the tunnel. Just before I plunged into the darkness, I looked back over my shoulder for one last time.

Aldo and Max had arrived at the edge of the platform and had come to a stop. They were staring after me helplessly. I could tell by their postures that they weren't going to follow. Like all New York City residents, they were fearful of dark subway tunnels.

As it happened, so was I. But the situation was different for me; I was running for my life. So I sprinted blindly through the darkness, running uptown on the downtown local tracks, hoping that I could reach the next station, almost a half mile away, before a train appeared and came at me head-on. I had a feeling I wouldn't make it.

I felt the vibrations first. Then there was a muted rumble that began to swell into a roar. I stopped and looked around desperately. It was so dark I could barely see the sides of the tunnel, but I had the impression it was frighteningly narrow. There was a chance that if I pressed myself against a wall the train would pass without touching me, but I was in too much of a panic to put that supposition to the test.

I noticed a crack of light a few yards up ahead. There was a niche in the wall at that spot, I realized, one of the lit recesses that were set in the sides of the tunnel at regular intervals, strategically placed points of retreat for the track workmen.

I ran forward. I got to the niche just as the train appeared, looming up before me seemingly out of nowhere. The glare of its headlight blinded me briefly. I threw myself into the niche and kept absolutely still as the roar, the stench and the filthy hot air passed over me in a wave.

When the train had gone, I relaxed. But only for a moment. Suddenly I realized that I was no longer holding the manila envelope. At some point in the frantic last minute, I had dropped it.

I stepped out to the edge of the niche and looked back in the direction from which I had come, peering into the murkiness of the tunnel, despairing of being able to find that envelope again.

Then, glancing down, I saw with relief that the envelope was lying at my feet. There was no need for me to run at top speed now. For once I could be grateful for the

deterioration of the New York subway system. I knew
from past experience that no other Lexington Avenue
local would come along for some time.

And so I trotted easily the rest of the way to the
Fifty-first Street station.

When I was above ground again, I sought out a large
public place where I could sit undisturbed. After walking
a block or two in the East Fifties, I found what I was
looking for—a cafeteria that was half empty, becalmed in
the mid-morning lull.

I entered, went through the line at the counter to get
a cup of coffee, then sat at a table in the rear. Carefully
I started opening the envelope.

I had decided that I had to do this. Whatever was in
that envelope was highly important to Edgar Greville and
his associates, so important that it had justified shooting
Desmond Corley. And it would have been a double shooting if I had been a little less quick on my feet.

It was possible that the contents of the envelope were
as Marisa had described them—photographs that proved
that her husband had been murdered. But in that case,
what had just happened seemed excessive. Was it normal
for New York gangsters to gun down a man in broad
daylight simply to protect some obscure thugs in faraway
Italy?

I had accepted Marisa's story when she had told it to
me. And I had accepted the idea that Edgar Greville was
determined to suppress the evidence of Peter Winfield's
murder so that there would be no scandal that might
endanger his sale of *The Etruscan Dancer* to the Metropolitan.

But now I was starting to wonder about it. Marisa had

portrayed Desmond Corley as a friend who was helping her selflessly. That wasn't, however, the impression I had gotten from him. After being with Corley for a minute or two, I had felt certain—not from anything tangible but as a matter of intuition—that he was no white knight in pursuit of justice. He had been out to make some score of his own.

Well, there was no point in speculating about Corley now. I was holding the answer to the puzzle in my hands. I had come within one step of death for the sake of what was in that envelope. I felt I had earned the right to an early look.

The flap of the manila envelope had been securely fastened with pieces of paper tape, and it took me awhile to open it without damaging it. Finally I pulled back the flap and slipped out the thin stack of eight-by-ten photographs that was within.

The top photograph both surprised me and puzzled me. It was a picture of a clay figure, and for a second, I didn't know what it was. Then I recognized it as *The Etruscan Dancer*. The figure was complete, but the surface was unfinished; the exotic features weren't fully defined yet. What was it? Had somebody for some reason done a clay copy of the old Etruscan statue?

The next photograph showed *The Etruscan Dancer* again, complete and in bronze but looking very new, with no signs of age on it.

In the photograph after that, this pristine *Etruscan Dancer* was lying in a huge bathtub filled with liquid. It was a downward shot and it showed the whole of the figure, with its akimbo arms, angled carefully so that all of it was immersed in the liquid. Wires extended into the bathtub, as if in preparation for releasing an electric charge into the liquid.

In the last photograph, I saw *The Etruscan Dancer* as it now was—discolored, with a patina of great age to it, looking thousands of years old.

I took out several sheets of paper from the envelope. Chemical formulae were on them, written in pencil. There were percentages and weights, rendered as milligrams per gram, of various minerals such as iron, lead and arsenic.

I didn't need to look at what was on these pages too closely. I knew what it all added up to. A recipe for forgery.

I understood it now, understood the whole story from its beginnings in Italy until that moment as I sat in that cafeteria. And, as in a detective novel, I should have been elated that I had solved the mystery at last.

But I felt no triumph. Instead, there was a sense of emptiness in me—the emptiness that is left after a dream has evaporated.

I thought of Marisa, but not joyfully, as I had earlier that morning, not in terms of the promise of future happiness. I thought of her now as she fit into the solution of the problem.

And putting my hand over my eyes, I wanted to cry.

15

I rang the bell. Almost immediately, I heard Marisa's quick, light step within.

When she opened the door, I saw that she was wearing her purchase of the morning. It was a canary-blue sheath, cut low at the neck. It made her seem, in the frame of mind I was in, punishingly beautiful.

"Where have you been?" she asked agitatedly. "It's two o'clock. I've been worried!"

"I was detained," I said.

I entered the apartment, closing the door almost shut after me. But not completely; I left it open an inch.

"Did something happen?" she asked.

"Yes, I'm afraid so."

I was steeling myself to break the tragic news to her. But Marisa showed no further curiosity about it. Instead, she looked down at the manila envelope in my hand. "Good," she said, "you have it." She snatched the envelope from me eagerly and turned away to study it more closely.

Now that her attention was elsewhere, I flipped the switch on the inside lock. Then I silently pushed the door into place, leaving it closed but unlocked.

Marisa was inspecting the envelope at length, as if she was a little uneasy about it. I had done my best to seal it again, putting all the bits of tape back onto the flap. But it still looked as if it might have been opened.

Her behavior struck me as odd. She was focusing on the envelope, and at the same time, she seemed to have completely forgotten about the man who had brought it to this country.

Finally I mentioned him. "Aren't you going to ask me about Desmond Corley?"

"Oh, yes," she said, turning back to me. "Where is he?"

"He's dead," I replied. "They killed him."

Marisa hardly reacted at all. The expression of distress came to her face quickly, but it seemed to be indicated rather than felt. "Oh—that's terrible," she murmured.

I looked at her perplexedly for a moment. "You don't seem too surprised," I said. "And I thought you'd be more upset."

"She *is* a little upset, Mr. Mercer," a voice said, "but not surprised."

I turned. Edgar Greville was standing in the doorway to the bedroom. He stepped into the living room. Aldo and Max emerged from the bedroom and joined him. They stood on either side of Greville and kept their gazes fixed on me. Their eyes were baleful, as if, after the hard time I had given them, they were looking forward to settling accounts with me.

"You see," Greville went on, "we've told her about it already."

Greville looked even more elegant than the last time I had seen him. He was wearing a pearl-gray suit with a three-point violet handkerchief in the breast pocket, and two-tone wingtip shoes. As he stood there, he had a dandyish arrogance to his posture. Before, he had been merely self-assured. Now he seemed supremely self-confident, as if everything had worked out completely to his satisfaction.

"How did you find her?" I asked him.

"We didn't," Greville said. "She contacted us. She decided it was time to make her peace with us."

"You mean, she's decided to stop trying to blackmail you?" I turned to Marisa. "That's right, isn't it, Marisa? That *is* what you were doing? Threatening to reveal the fact that *The Etruscan Dancer* is a forgery?"

Marisa gazed at me calmly for a moment. "I don't call it blackmail," she said.

"It's the word that's generally used."

"It was negotiation." Her voice was cold and hard. "For my husband's fair share."

"He wasn't paid properly?"

"Of course not! It was Peter who forged *The Etruscan Dancer.* No one else could have done it. He had the sculptor's skill. And he was the only one who knew the exact chemical composition of Etruscan bronze." Angrily she said, "And they paid him a pittance!"

"My dear girl," Greville said, "a deal is a deal. Peter had to abide by the terms."

"Maybe *he* did," Marisa said. "But *I* didn't have to."

"And your greediness almost cost you your life," Greville said.

I noticed his use of the past tense. "She'll be all right now?" I asked him.

"Thanks to *your* interference." He gazed at me with a mixture of annoyance and regret. I had the feeling that he would have greatly preferred the initially intended outcome. "You've called too much attention to this affair.

It's now inadvisable for us to carry out our original plan."

"You were going to lure Desmond Corley into delivering this into your hands"—I pointed to the envelope that Marisa was holding—"the proof of the forgery. And then—?"

"We don't need to verbalize it," Greville said. "Let's just say that you've accomplished your purpose. You've saved this wretched woman's life." Dryly he added, "If you knew her as well as I do, you might not consider it such a service to humanity."

"And have I helped her get what she wanted?" I asked.

"Not as much as she originally demanded," he replied. "But she'll end up doing quite nicely."

I looked at Marisa again. "How much of the take are you getting?"

"Discussing money is vulgar, isn't it, darling," she said, "for two people who have been as close as we have?"

Her mocking smile chilled me. I couldn't believe that she was the beautiful, loving girl I had held in my arms the night before. That gentle girl was gone and in her place was this icy, contemptuous, predatory woman.

Greville answered my question. "She'll be richer by a quarter of a million dollars—once that envelope is delivered to me. And you've been so kind as to bring it." He went to Marisa and took the envelope from her. He turned to me. "I assume you've checked through this already?"

"It's all there," I said.

My word, evidently, wasn't good enough. He quickly tore open the envelope, removed the photographs and looked at them one after the other.

When he had finished inspecting the pictures, I asked, "Did Peter Winfield take those?"

"Yes."

"Why?"

"Vanity, I suppose," Greville said as he slipped the photographs back into the envelope. He looked at Marisa. "Wouldn't you say so?"

She nodded. "Vanity," she said, "and bitterness. Peter was bitter because the world hadn't recognized him as a sculptor. He knew that *The Etruscan Dancer* would be acclaimed as a masterpiece. He wanted to be able to prove someday that it was his own work. That, for Peter, would have been the supreme joke."

"Yes, it would have been very amusing," Greville said. "But we'll have to deny Peter his little laugh—wherever he is." He held up the envelope. "This is about to go into the incinerator."

The statement had finality to it, and the matter seemed settled. Suddenly there was silence in the room. All four of them were looking at me now, and they all had the same intent gleam in their eyes.

Uneasily I said, "Well, I guess everything's worked out fine for everybody."

"Not for everybody, Mr. Mercer," Greville said. "You've put us in an awkward position. *You* know the story. And we can't allow you to tell it."

I pondered this for a moment, even though his words didn't require analysis. Their meaning was abundantly clear.

"Murder doesn't impress you much, does it, Mr. Greville?" I said.

Aldo spoke up suddenly. "You got no complaints, buddy," he said. "You've been living on borrowed time. I should have iced you at the Seaview Inn."

"Yes, I can see where you might feel that way," I said mildly.

I was choosing my words carefully, trying to keep the conversation going. I knew that this scene wasn't what it seemed to be, and that in theory I was in no great danger. I had been dumb enough in the last few days. I hadn't been so dumb that I had come back to this apartment unprepared.

A microphone was taped to my chest, and outside in the hallway, a police lieutenant named Michalski, along with two other detectives, was listening to this conversation. The whole setup had been arranged swiftly, within two hours of the time I had gone to the police. The murder in Grand Central Station, plus the story I had had to tell, had been more than enough to make this a top-priority case.

But we had thought that I would be recording Marisa alone; we hadn't expected the presence of these three homicidally inclined men. And so now the situation was more ticklish. At any second, something could go wrong. A swift, murderous action—as swift as the killing of Desmond Corley had been—and all preparations, all precautions would become meaningless.

"I guess this is it," I said to Greville. "But I still have my novelist's curiosity. So, if you don't mind, I'd appreciate it if you'd clear up a couple of points for me."

He arched his eyebrows, as if he thought my continued interest, in the circumstances, a bit peculiar. "Such as what?"

I turned to Marisa now. "Who engineered your husband's death?" I asked. "Who tampered with his car?"

"Desmond Corley did," she answered.

"Why did he do it?"

"Because I asked him to."

"Was it really necessary?"

"When you have a weak idiot for a husband," Marisa said, "it's necessary."

"He wouldn't go along with your blackmail plan?"

"He said he had a sense of honor about it. Can you imagine? An honorable forger! Anyway," she added, "I would have had to choose between Desmond and him sooner or later. And Desmond was better in bed."

"Oh." I considered this new revelation. That morning I would have felt a twinge of jealousy, but now I simply assessed it with professional interest. "Guilty sex. This story has needed that."

"I needed it, too," she said. "I'll miss Desmond." There was a very faint regret in her voice. "But the quarter of a million should be some compensation." She smiled. "Has this worked out like one of your *schlock* books, Hank?"

"Actually," I said, "it's a little like *The Maltese Falcon.*"

"I love that movie," she said.

"But it's different, too," I went on. "Sam Spade didn't have the advantages of modern technology."

Marisa looked blank. Greville, however, picked up on it at once. "What do you mean by *that?*" he asked sharply.

The others were alert now. Their intense, suspicious gazes burned into me and I suddenly felt embarrassingly exposed, as if I were stripped to the waist and the microphone on my chest visible.

I was growing very nervous. I had meant my last comment as a cue line for Lieutenant Michalski, a signal to him to make his move. But nothing was happening. With rising panic, I wondered if the microphone had stopped working.

Aldo rushed over to me, grabbed me by the arm and patted my chest. "This guy is wired!" he said loudly, with consternation.

That, it turned out, was the real cue Lieutenant Michalski had needed. The door flew open and Michalski and the two other detectives burst into the room with their guns drawn. "Freeze!" Michalski shouted.

Everything happened very fast at that point. The automatic appeared in Aldo's hand almost instantly, and I saw that Max was drawing his gun, too. Aldo was the only one of them who got off a shot. The return fire of the detectives was prompt and accurate.

I heard it rather than witnessed it, since the moment I saw the pistol in Aldo's hand, I dove facedown onto the floor.

My nose was to the carpet, but I had the blurred impression of Aldo collapsing to the floor, quite near me on my left. He dropped and lay absolutely still. In another part of the room, Max was moaning with pain.

At almost the same time, in the seconds immediately after Aldo fell, there was a commotion at the door. I heard a scuffling and then a cry of anger from Marisa.

I turned onto my side and looked back over my right shoulder. All three detectives were surrounding Marisa and Greville. Evidently, during the exchange of gunshots, they had tried to dart out the doorway. They hadn't been quick enough, and now the detectives had a firm grip on them. Marisa and Greville seemed very depressed.

The whole business, from the time Michalski had yelled "Freeze!" had taken no more than ten or fifteen seconds. And everything—or so I thought—was satisfactorily concluded. I started to push myself up to a sitting position.

Biff Deegan suddenly appeared, kneeling beside me on my right. With an agitated look on his face, he pointed past me. "Hank!" he cried out. "Behind you!"

I whirled around.

Aldo was still lying on the floor. But his eyes were open and he was staring at me with hatred. His hand had found his automatic again and, very weakly, with the last bit of strength he had left, he was slowly raising it to point it at me.

I grabbed Aldo's wrist and in the same motion fell backward. The gun went off.

Looking up from the floor, I saw Biff recoil, grimace with pain and clutch at his chest. It was only a moment's glimpse of him. All my concentration was on Aldo. I rolled toward him to struggle with him.

But there was no need. Aldo's hand went limp and the gun dropped to the floor. His eyes closed and he sank back, no longer a threat, simply an unconscious, badly wounded man with a bloodstain spreading on his shirt front.

I turned quickly and looked at Biff. He was lying on his back, with the porkpie hat tipped over his eyes. His chest was still; he wasn't breathing.

I stared at him dully. Then the realization came to me. Biff had taken the bullet that had been intended for me. Now he was dead.

Lieutenant Michalski rushed over. He picked up the pistol, straightened up again, looked down at the unconscious Aldo and then at me. His relief was clear on his face.

"That was a close call," he said. "Your guardian angel was watching over you *that* time."

I looked to my side again. But there was nothing there now. Biff was gone.

I couldn't help myself; I let out a cry. A cry of anguish. Of grief.

16

I had delivered on my promise to Norman. It was a page-one story and then some. There was the big front-page article in the *New York Times* when the story of *The Etruscan Dancer* conspiracy broke. And then the tabloids got another week out of it as further arrests were made.

Marisa and Greville, of course, were already in detention, and Aldo and Max were in the hospital, recovering from their wounds. But four other people were unearthed who had been in on the New York end of the conspiracy. Three of them were underworld figures whose names were unfamiliar to me, and the fourth was Gary Halloran. Halloran's girl friend, Carolee, wasn't among those arraigned. She was to be spared an indictment, since she had agreed to be a witness for the state.

All in all, it had turned out to be as notorious a case as any book editor could have desired. And Norman was particularly genial when I met with him at his office to discuss our new book.

"Perry is asking for the moon on this one," Norman said. He chuckled indulgently, as if, in the mood he was in, he could tolerate anything, even an agent's rapacious greed. "Something will be worked out, I'm sure. But we shouldn't be distracted by these crass matters. We should just go ahead and get started on the book."

I didn't say anything. As a rule, I didn't discuss negotiations with my editor. But beyond that, the way I was feeling, I didn't know what I wanted to say about anything else, either. I had been in a funk the past few days.

"Now, ideally," Norman went on, "this should be a nonfiction book—the real story, just the way it happened. But you're a novelist, and I'm not going to ask you to learn how to use a whole different set of muscles at this late date. So we'll do it the way you want it—as your first Amos Frisby book."

"I don't think so," I said.

He looked at me uncertainly. "You don't think what?"

"I don't think I want to do it. I don't want to write the book."

Norman's face froze in an expression of shock. Even *I* was a little surprised. I had sensed it was where my thought processes had been leading me. But I hadn't expected to make up my mind so swiftly or that I would be able to say it so easily.

"I don't understand," Norman said. "You promised me a big book. *This* is the big book."

"Maybe. But I'm not ready to write it yet."

"If you don't write this, what *are* you going to write?"

"I want to do another Biff Deegan," I said.

He took a moment to absorb this. The faint look of astonishment didn't vanish from his face, but I could tell he wasn't really distressed by the idea.

At length, he asked, "What about Amos Frisby?"

"Amos Frisby is a fool," I said.

Norman nodded, as if I was confirming his own impression of Frisby. But he wasn't ready yet to give up on his hot-off-the-front-pages blockbuster. "What about *The Etruscan Dancer?*" he asked. "Are you *ever* going to tell that story?"

"Someday. But, for now, I'm sticking with Biff Deegan."

I had said it with a finality that left him no choice about it. With a resigned sigh, he said, "All right, if this is what you want to do, I won't stand in your way."

"Thanks, Norman."

"But I'm totally confused. Before you said you were through with Biff Deegan. So why do you want to write another Biff Deegan book now?"

The emotion welled up in me. "To preserve his memory," I said.

Norman stared at me. "What?"

I rose. "See you, Norman."

When I got outside, I walked in the general direction of the Village, but without pattern, almost aimlessly. I turned corners, chose side streets at random. It didn't seem to matter where I was or in what direction I was going. I was drifting, in these streets as in my life. I had never felt more alone.

And it was my fault. I had had a friend and I hadn't valued him. I had had someone who loved me, in his rough way, and I had been ashamed of him. I had rejected him.

And he had given his life for me.

I could keep his name alive in my books. I could make up more stories for him, giving him what shadowy existence fictional heroes had. But I would be doing it entirely on my own, working in a void, drawing only on my memory of him. It wouldn't be the same. It couldn't be the same.

I had been walking for some time with my head down, and I hardly knew where I was. I glanced to both sides now to get my bearings. I was on a gloomy side street in the commercial part of the West Twenties. A truck was unloading across the street, but otherwise, the street was quiet and there were few people around.

Then I looked ahead and stopped suddenly.

Biff Deegan was standing in the center of the sidewalk, a few yards away, smiling at me. His left arm was bandaged and in a sling.

I stared at him, stunned. Then, joyfully, I cried out, "Biff!"

I ran toward him. For a moment, I was afraid that he would disappear before I got to him. But he held firm, the whole tangible two-hundred-and-ten-pound bulk of him.

"God, am I glad to see you!" I said.

I was about to hug him happily, but he stepped back. "Easy," he said, touching his wounded left arm.

"Oh—sorry." I took him in wonderingly. "I can't believe it! You're alive!"

"Sure I'm alive," Biff said. "It would take a hell of a lot more than *that* to kill me."

We started walking down the street together. Neither of us said anything for a while. There were a thousand things I wanted to say to him, but for the moment, it seemed enough just to enjoy his massive, comforting presence beside me.

At length, Biff said, "I understand we're going to be working together again."

"Yeah," I said. "And this time we'll do it in style— down in some Caribbean resort—with lots of broads in bikinis."

"Hey, now you're talking!" he said.

We were silent again. Biff had yet to mention what had happened. He had every right to chide me for my recent stupidity. But he hadn't—nor, I realized now, was he going to. He was being generous and forgiving about it.

Still, I felt I owed him some kind of apology.

"I'm sorry," I said. "I'm sorry I made such a fool of myself—with Marisa Winfield."

"That's all right," Biff said. "You just gotta know who your real friends are."

He was right, of course. I *did* know, finally, and we could start fresh.

We walked on, side by side, on toward the future, with all its violent, perilous adventures. We were ready for it—ready for anything—now that we were together again.